BLOODY ATTACK

O'Brien left his Sharps on its tripod and started out toward the dead shaggy he'd just shot. But, just as he approached the animal, five big, gray timber wolves appeared over a nearby rise. Their eyes narrowing as they stared hungrily at him and his kill, O'Brien knew he'd have to stand and fight.

He grabbed his .38 Dardick from under his heavy bearcoat and yelled. "Get the hell out of here!" But the wolves began to circle him, growling deeply.

The buffalo hunter aimed and shot the nearest wolf in the head. The big animal sprang into the air, twisted then fell down dead in the snow. A second leaped at him from his blind side, knocking him down with weight.

O'Brien got off two more shots. One grazed the snarling beast and the other caught him square in the gut. Yelping and kicking, the wolf fell back onto the cold ground, dripping blood.

REVENGE
OF THE
BUFFALO
HUNTER

RALPH HAYES

PINNACLE BOOKS
WINDSOR PUBLISHING CORP.

PINNACLE BOOKS

are published by

Windsor Publishing Corp.
475 Park Avenue South
New York, NY 10016

First printing: February, 1992

Printed in the United States of America

Chapter One

Men like O'Brien had excelled at hunting almost from the earliest beginnings of time, in the dim recesses of prehistory, when they stumbled out of some Olduvai swamp, red-eyed and hostile, looking for trouble. Unlike the prowling lions and bears that roamed those steaming landscapes before the dawn of civilization, man had learned early on to seize the nearest sharp stick, track down his quarry with a remorseless and cunning intelligence, and then kill with a deadly tool fashioned with his own hands.

O'Brien had heard all that from an illiterate father whose life had been taken up almost entirely with tracking and hunting in the Shenandoan, a hill man who deemed it important to pass on to his male offspring those skills that were to him the most precious a man could possess. He had sat for hours with a very young O'Brien, alone at a creek bank or on some craggy hilltop, and in a gravelly voice related how vital hunting had been to men for time beyond reckoning, and how they had long ago come head to head with the big cat in a life-or-death competition for available game and, ultimately, for species domination, and how in the end it was the two-legged predator that emerged from that struggle for survival, thick-browed and dangerous, as the most efficient hunter the world had ever known.

His father had been taken down with the diphtheria when O'Brien was still short of puberty, and the disease had carried him off. It fell to O'Brien and a rather sickly mother to care for two younger sisters. O'Brien hunted the hills daily then to help his family survive, and by sixteen he was the best shot in the county and could track like a Comanche. When the family moved farther east later to live with an uncle in Maryland, O'Brien headed in the other direction on his own. He rode the Union Pacific to Oklahoma and then drifted on into Colorado territory, trying to find out what to do with his life. He did some droving for a while and then worked for several years with a trapping company. Finally, when he heard that buffalo hunting was becoming big business, he had turned to that occupation as his chosen life profession. He had run onto an old-timer named McGraw who taught him the refinements of hunting buffalo as opposed to other game, and their paths had crossed and recrossed over recent years, through the good times of hunting the "shaggies." Now, the big hide markets were playing out because the enormous herds of the old days were gone, and O'Brien and McGraw had joined up once again, just a few months previously, to pool their skills in locating the remaining good herds.

O'Brien realized he had missed the best days on the Great Plains, though. Men had been hunting the shaggies for meat, for sport, and for a dollar a hide since about 1830. In those days the buff were so thick on the plains that a man could ride through a herd all day and not come to the end of it. Fancy-clothed rich men from Europe came over just to hunt for trophies, and they always wanted to take home a few bison robes. There had been quite a ceremony to the hunt in those days, McGraw had told O'Brien once. Someone tossed a feather into the air to test the wind and ritually begin the hunt, and then the whole party would begin what they called "stripping." They would rid themselves and their mounts of all unnecessary gear before charging into the fray. With sleeves rolled up and kerchiefs tied across their foreheads, they would ride into a herd at full gallop, sometimes on an expensive Arabian stallion, with cartridges stuck into pockets, sashes, and even their mouths. When the herd started running, they could not hear the sound of their own guns firing, so raucous was the thunder of the hooves around them.

It had been somewhat like that when O'Brien first got into it. But now, in his mid-thirties, O'Brien knew that buffalo hunting would not last forever. So he had partnered up with McGraw again to try to make the hunting more efficient while it lasted. McGraw, over fifty now, was very much like O'Brien. They both liked living out in the open, disliked having to visit towns where there were jails and churches and rules, and were most content when they were out on the hoot-owl trails, setting up hardship camp, eating soda biscuits from a flour sack, and boiling chicory coffee in a tomato can.

Now, on this bitter winter morning of February of 1881, in the southern hills of Colorado Territory, O'Brien huddled up against a snow-covered stump and studied the scene that lay before him. McGraw had guessed right, they were there. About fifty shaggies, standing belly deep in glistening snow, chewing their cuds into a soft but frigid northwest breeze, narrow fountains of steam regularly rising from their wet nostrils. A young spike bull turned toward O'Brien and stared right at him, but then looked away. O'Brien had once seen a George Catlin painting in the lobby of a Dodge City hotel that depicted such a panorama. But, looking at the painting, you could not feel the ice in your fingers and legs, nor hear the soft grunting of the cows as they fed on the dead grass that lanced through the surface of the snow at their feet, and you could not smell the sweet stink of the animals as the breeze brought it upwind.

It was always more difficult to find buffalo in the winter, but this year it had been worse than ever. Five years ago O'Brien would not have bothered with a small herd like this one. Large herds produced quality hides. Most hides were used for utilitarian purposes, but a flawless hide with a rich color would bring a premium dollar on

8

the marketplace. These so-called robes, named that way because Indians had worn them for clothing, were made into expensive rugs or wall hangings in civilized places, and hunters had been killed for good ones. In fact, McGraw had recently confided to O'Brien that one reason he was still out here "busting every rise on his belly, like a goddam snake" was a persistent rumor that a great albino buffalo had been spotted on a number of occasions in this territory, always with a different herd, and that it was an animal of such snow-white perfection and tremendous size that its robe would bring almost any price that a lucky hunter would care to ask for it.

O'Brien glanced to his right where, fifty yards away in a shallow depression in the snow, McGraw lay on his belly, a dark hulk against the purity of the snow who looked every bit as wild and primordial as the animals on the rise of ground just above them. McGraw's breath came out in frosty spurts as he moistened a finger and held it up head high, to make sure they were still downwind from the herd. He turned to O'Brien and nodded.

O'Brien hefted the Sharps custom-made double-barreled rifle he held in cold hands and returned the nod. McGraw held a similiar weapon, but an older model. They both took aim on the herd, going for the oldest bulls at which they could get a clear shot. Their mounts were picketed two hundred yards behind them in a stand of gnarled pines. You did not use horses to ride into a winter herd in deep snow. You shot from the perimeter and hoped you could bring down a half-dozen animals before the herd galloped out of range.

O'Brien sighted in on the biggest bull he could see clearly, took in a deep breath, and held it. In the next moment the tranquillity of the mountain scene was destroyed in a violent eruption of explosions, as first O'Brien's gun went off, then McGraw's. Each man fired both barrels, and four big shaggies crumpled where they stood. But now the herd began running as the men reloaded, and after a moment of indecision, not understanding from where the shots had come, the animals headed right at the hunters, not seeing them.

O'Brien had had this happen to him before and knew how dangerous it could be. Now the small herd was thundering right down on him and McGraw. O'Brien threw his rifle down and flattened himself behind the stump, and a big cow stampeded past him, its red eyes looking wild. A hoof grazed O'Brien's arm and tore the rawhide coat in which he was bundled. He hunkered lower, and other animals rioted past, making a loud racket. Out of the corner of his eye, he saw McGraw break the most basic rule and rise to run out of their way.

"Stay down!" O'Brien shouted at his partner. He had had other evidence recently that McGraw in his middle age was losing some of his cold-steel nerves required to do this for a living. Now he had allowed panic to seize him. "Goddam it, McGraw, get—"

In the middle of his command, a young bull, the

same one O'Brien had noted earlier, ran right into McGraw.

McGraw went flying, his rifle knocked from his grasp. The rest of the herd roared on past, but the young bull stopped and turned to his fallen enemy. As O'Brien grabbed his now-loaded rifle up again, the bull struck at McGraw with its horns, hitting him in the thigh. O'Brien saw McGraw wince in pain as he was pulled off the ground and dumped back down again in a broken position. O'Brien yanked the big sixteen-pound Sharps up and sighted on the bull, just as it set itself to gore McGraw again. This time, O'Brien figured, McGraw would catch one of those horns in his rib cage, and that would probably be fatal. The buffalo lowered its shaggy head to attack again, and O'Brien fired, hitting the buffalo just behind the foreleg. The animal raised his head, shuddered, and fell onto its side right beside McGraw, one of its hooves kicking him in the side as it fell. It quivered on the ground and was dead.

O'Brien rose. The herd was gone now, and silence moved in again. Steam rose from the ground where the buffalo lay beside McGraw. O'Brien walked over to his partner in shallow snow and looked down on him. Uphill from them, four other dead buffalo lay against the snow, two of them with their legs in the air, mouths open, eyes staring.

McGraw looked up at O'Brien and grinned sheepishly. "Sorry," he gritted out. He was a blocky, heavy man wearing a bear robe and a raccoon cap. He had a grizzled gray beard, a beefy face, and eyes that showed years of squinting into the glare of harsh sun.

O'Brien nodded and knelt beside McGraw. His rawhide trousers were torn, and there was quite a lot of blood, crimson on the snow. "I don't think he broke the bone," O'Brien said.

"I don't know why I did that," McGraw apologized. "I saw a man with his skull crushed by buff couple of years ago. I never forgot it. Sometimes I think I ain't got it in me anymore for this kind of shit."

O'Brien took a big bowie knife from a stovepipe boot and began cutting McGraw's trouser leg away from the big wound. "We got to get you bandaged up, or you're a dead man."

"Just get me to my mount, and I'll be okay till we get back to camp," McGraw said, grunting it out.

"Just shut up, goddam it," O'Brien growled. He was a tall, muscular man, athletic-looking with a rawboned face and deep blue eyes. The few women who ever got a look at him considered him ruggedly handsome, but O'Brien had never gotten close enough to one to really know what they were like, except in bed. He wore an abbreviated handlebar mustache, and his darkish hair was almost shoulder length. Underneath the skin coat he wore rawhides, and there was a trail-colored Stetson atop his head.

McGraw gave O'Brien a look and clammed up. You didn't argue with O'Brien. In towns all over the territory, men had learned the hard way that O'Brien was left better unprovoked. O'Brien got a bandana out of a pocket and tied it around the wound in McGraw's thigh to stop the bleeding. Then he took a thong of rawhide from a belt wallet and applied a tourniquet above the wound.

"I don't know what got into me," McGraw mumbled.

O'Brien helped the blocky man up, and they headed for the dun mare picketed to a pine tree, near O'Brien's Appaloosa stallion, McGraw hobbling along, leaning on O'Brien. "Good thing I waren't alone," McGraw mumbled. "Shit, how dumb can you get."

"Forget it," O'Brien told him.

O'Brien helped him aboard the mare, then threw the reins over the saddlehorn. He pulled at an edge of yellow long underwear that showed at his neck, because he was sweating now in the cold. Then he trudged through the snow to his Appaloosa, a few yards away. He slid the Sharps into a saddle scabbard on the mount's irons and pulled a ground sheet out of his blanket roll behind the saddle.

"You ride on back to camp down below. I'm going to skin them shaggies and bring them on back."

McGraw nodded, hunkering dejectedly in his saddle. "I guess I'm just getting too old for this."

O'Brien did not reply to that. He seldom spoke more than was necessary to communicate on a basic level. He hated to talk anything to death. McGraw spurred his mare and moved off, his leather creaking under his pressure.

O'Brien spent the next hour or so on the dead

13

buffalo. There was one excellent, robe-quality hide, and he skinned head and all because the Fort Garland market liked them that way. He would slit the skin down the belly from the throat to the root of the tail, and down the inside of each leg to the knee. Then he staked the head of each animal to the ground by driving a wagon rod through the nose into the ground. After that he tied a hitch of rope to a thick wad of hide on the back of the neck, fastened the other end to the Appaloosa's saddle-horn, and guided the horse away, ripping the skin off the buffalo. The hides were then wrapped in the ground sheet and packed aboard the mount, and before he left, O'Brien stripped tallow off a couple of the heaviest animals, for cooking grease, and then cut a few steaks for grub.

Back at camp later, it was late morning, and McGraw had a fire going outside their tent. He seemed to be feeling all right, but O'Brien knew he needed medical help. That meant giving up this hunt and taking McGraw to Fort Garland, a two-day's ride away. O'Brien staked their hides out in the sun. He opened up some beans for them, then heated up some coffee over the fire. They sat on a log then, eating quietly.

"You're right," McGraw finally said, when he threw the empty beans can down beside the fire. "I'll go. I think I need some time off, anyway. But that means you'll have to ride alone."

"I've done it before," O'Brien said. It had been McGraw's idea to ride out together again a few months ago. O'Brien had become a loner since their last meeting, though, and had had to give the

14

suggestion a lot of thought.

"There ain't much use in this till spring, anyway," McGraw said, squinting his deep-set eyes at O'Brien. His cheeks had a rosy glow in this temperature. "I'll rest easy in town for a while, living fat. About March I'd like to head south. That big albino was seen just a few weeks ago down east of the Chaco. Wouldn't I just like to get my sights on that animal."

O'Brien swigged the last of his coffee. He looked upon the white buffalo rumors as a will-o'-the-wisp fantasy by some drunken hunter that liked drinking more than tracking.

"A man can't plan his hunting around one animal," he finally said in a deep voice. He ran fingers through the brown mustache. "I knew a trapper when I was working for the Western Furs outfit. Had a thing about this big grizzly. Had a dream about shooting that bear in the left eye and selling the pelt for big money. Trouble was, that bear was an ornery sonofabitch that had killed three men already. One day the trapper found the bear way up high on a mountainside. He put a bullet in the bear's left eye, and it didn't go down. Then he put one in its chest and one in its belly. The bear knocked him down, gutted him, tore his head off, and then run off. Nobody ever found that bear."

McGraw glanced over at him and grinned. "That's some story, O'Brien. That mean you won't go south with me later?"

O'Brien hunched wide shoulders. "I don't know where I'll be in March, McGraw," he said. "But I

15

won't be out scouring the hills for no white buffalo." He threw the dregs of the coffee into the fire and it sizzled there. "Matter of fact, I heard a friend of mine from back home is down in Stinking Creek. I think I'll maybe take some time off, too, and go see him."

"Didn't know you had any friends," McGraw said, grinning.

O'Brien let a small smile move the corner of his mouth. "Aaron Seger come from the same neck of the woods as me. Got a little girl now, I hear, but he's widowed. Years ago, it was Aaron that brought me the news that my family had all been buried with the influenza."

McGraw looked over and saw a somber look edge across O'Brien's face like a black thunderhead. "Thought I owed it to Aaron to pay my respects. Might not ever get the chance again."

McGraw nodded. Over at the picket rope, one of the horses whinnied softly. "Sounds right, O'Brien. Maybe you and me will meet up down south somewhere in the good weather. You might change your mind about the white buffalo."

O'Brien's face lightened up some again. "Not likely," he said. He looked over toward their hide wagon that stood over at the edge of camp. A long-eared mule was still hitched to it, looking asleep. "You're going to need that wagon. When we sell them hides in Fort Garland, I'll let you buy me out for your share of the profit."

"Why, they won't hardly bring enough," McGraw said.

O'Brien shrugged. "If we meet up again down

around the Chaco, you can let me back in cheap."

McGraw grunted. A fair-minded hunter was as rare as a banker in heaven, but O'Brien would stand by a man he respected till hell froze over, and then skate around on the ice a while.

"You sure you got to go to Stinking Creek?" he offered.

O'Brien nodded. "I been going to do this for quite a spell. There ain't many men I'd ride for over a day to see, but Aaron's the exception. No, I'm going."

"Well, I hope it's worth the trip," McGraw said.

"There ain't no way it won't be," O' Brien replied.

They both rose from the log, and McGraw grimaced with pain in the leg. "Well, I guess I better get to Fort Garland before this leg begins thinking gangrene," he said.

"You find yourself a good horse doctor," O'Brien said. "He can sew that up real good for you and he won't push no pills at you neither."

"I'll get along," McGraw said. "I got a couple of good hunts left in me."

O'Brien headed over to the skins to break them loose. "I just hope this territory has," he said.

Down south of where O'Brien and McGraw had been hunting, in the New Mexico Territory, a man quite different from O'Brien rode into the town of Lincoln on that winter morning when O'Brien was accompanying McGraw to Fort Garland. His name was Wesley Sumner, and he was a different sort of hunter. He went out for bounties on other men's heads, men who had busted the law in serious ways and who were successful in eluding capture and punishment.

It was almost as cold in Lincoln that morning as it was up north where O'Brien had skinned his buffalo. There wasn't much snow on the ground, but there was a nippy breeze out of the west that bit into a man's flesh and kept most locals indoors. Sumner walked his coal-black stallion down the main street of town slowly and stopped it before a weathered brick building with a sign out front that read, *Sheriff.* Up ahead a short distance, a heavily bundled middle-aged man hurried across the street into a store, braced against the light wind, but he was the only person on the street besides Sumner. Sumner dismounted from the big horse and swaddled the reins over a hitching post outside the entrance to the local jail. In his early thirties, Sumner was a six foot even, lithe-looking fellow with a handsome, aquiline face, dark hair, and dark brown eyes.

He was attired in a long riding coat with a corduroy jacket over a red vest under that, and a flowing blue cravat was tied loosely at his throat. He wore a dark wide-brimmed hat on his head, a Colt .45 Peacemaker on a cartridge belt under the coat and jacket, and a small one-shot derringer at the small of his back. Sumner was almost always neatly dressed, and drifters often mistook him for a New Orleans gambler when they spotted him in a bar. In fact, Sumner was good at cards, but it was not that skill that had earned him a name in the territory. An ex-convict, Sumner had spent a short hitch in prison for killing a man who had raped his aunt when Sumner was only fifteen. Later, he had chummed around with Clay Allison for a while, and he had had a brief drinking orgy with a young William Bonney a couple of years prior. It had been Clay Allison who had intimated that he had been glad he had never had to test himself against Sumner, and that started Sumner's big reputation with a gun. Then, when Sumner killed a lightning-fast killer named Curly Quentin not long ago in self-defense, his name had become feared throughout the territory. Along with Billy the Kid and Clay Allison, Sumner was considered unbeatable with a six-shooter. After the Quentin killing, he had been given a nickname that stuck to the present. He was known as "Certainty" Sumner, because, since he had gone into bounty hunting, a man was as good as dead when Sumner went after him. Nobody expected Sumner to bring a wanted man in alive, and he never did.

It was a heavily overcast morning, and there was an oil lamp burning inside the building, visible through a dusty window. Sumner walked up to the door, his spurs clinking dully over frozen mud, and pushed a heavy wood door open and moved through it.

A man sat behind a desk in the white-plastered room, reading a Kansas City newspaper that was two weeks old. He was a rather big man with a dark complexion and black mustache, and he was dressed in dungarees and a wool jacket that looked Indian. He was bare headed, with wild-looking, black hair, and a meerschaum pipe was clenched in his teeth. He looked up with a bored look, but then his expression changed.

"Well, I'll be a horn-swaggled sonofabitch. Certainty Sumner." He rose off his chair with a grin.

"Morning, Pat. God, you don't ever change." Sumner closed the door behind him and went over to extend his hand. The man who took it and pumped it enthusiastically was Pat Garrett, the sheriff in Lincoln and one of the most proficient gunslingers west of Kansas City. Raised in Louisiana, he had drifted west at an early age. Coincidentally, he had hunted for buffalo at one time and had met O'Brien at a skinning camp. It had been Garrett who had compared O'Brien to a grizzly and had said to another gunman that if anyone ever tried to kill O'Brien, he would have to put ten or twelve bullets in him and then club him for a while.

"You whelp of a wolf, you making any money?" Garrett said.

"You know how bounty tracking is," Sumner said in a smooth, well-modulated voice. His aunt had given him more schooling than some men ever got out there, and he talked like it. "If you got the time, Pat, I'll buy you a Red Top rye at that saloon across the street."

Garrett made a face. "It don't open for an hour. Anyway, my stomach's been acting up on me, Sumner. The local pill man says I got to cut back on the alcohol." He moved a chair out from the desk. "Take the weight off, my boy. I ain't had

20

nobody to talk with in three seasons."

They both sat down, and Sumner unbuttoned the long coat. Garrett threw his booted feet up onto the desk. Sumner removed the dark hat and laid it in front of him. "I see you've got the Kansas City news. Anything happening in the big world out there?"

"Well, Garfield was inaugurated," Garrett said. "I hope he takes this country up a hill, by Jesus. Then there's still that war going on in Africa. Them English got their asses kicked by the Boers at some place I can't pronounce. In London, they're going to have real electric lights in that Savoy Theater they're building. Can you fathom that?"

Sumner shook his head, smiling. "Sometimes it seems like it's all moving pretty fast out there."

"Too fast for me," Garrett said. "I can't even keep the law in my own county some days."

"It seems like there's plenty of work for both of us out there," Sumner told him. Garrett picked the pipe up from where he had laid it on the desk and knocked it out.

"I hear Wyatt Earp's got his hands full over in Tombstone, with the Clantons," Garrett said quietly. "I reckon that'll come to a head pretty soon, if I know Wyatt."

"He's a man that doesn't take much pushing," Sumner agreed. He had been through Earp's town recently, and Earp had asked Sumner to disarm himself while he was there. Sumner had acquiesced, and the whole town had breathed a sigh of relief. Unlike Garrett, Earp did not want bounty hunters

21

around, so Sumner had not stayed long.

"At least the James boys seem to have retired for a spell," Garrett said. "My trouble lately has been with small fry like your old friend Billy."

Sumner knew he was referring to his one-time drinking bout with Billy the Kid, at a time when Billy had not yet proven himself to be a cold-blooded murderer. "Bonney? He's no friend of mine, Pat. What's he up to now?"

Garrett shrugged. "He drew down on some punk kid east of here just before Christmas and killed him. Now I got to make sure he ain't in my county anymore."

Sumner nodded. "He's dangerous, Pat."

"I know." Garrett touched a six-shooter hanging on his belt. "I don't plan to play games with the bastard if I run into him."

"He won't play any with you," Sumner said. "He's back-shot a lot of people by now."

"He won't get no necktie party here," Garrett said. "Say, you want to look at some wanted dodgers?"

Sumner shook his head. "No, I know what I'm after, Pat." He pulled a paper from his coat pocket and handed it over the desk to Garrett. "I'm after the Gabriels."

Garrett frowned slightly, took the wanted dodger, and glanced at it. He nodded. "I know about them sonsofbitches,," he said. "There's five of them now. The brothers are running with three other men, all with dodgers on them."

Sumner grinned slightly. "That's what caught my attention. With the rewards on the brothers added to the smaller ones on the rest of the gang, I figure I could retire for a year on the proceeds."

Garrett handed the dodger back, and Sumner pocketed it. "If they don't kill you," Garrett said.

Sumner shrugged. "Nobody lives forever, Pat."

Garrett thought Sumner reminded him of himself when he was younger. Except he was never as good as Sumner. "You know anything about these people?" he said.

"A little," Sumner replied. "I've been on their trail for a few weeks now, getting information on them." He propped his leg on the desk. "They're in this area, Pat, but I don't know where. I thought you might be able to help me."

Garrett grunted. "They were seen over at Bernardo at a New Year's celebration. But that was a few weeks ago." He got up, walked over to a pot-bellied stove on the rear wall, and poked some embers up in it. He rubbed his hands in front of it. "I hope to hell they don't come here." He looked over at Sumner. "You ever hear that rumor about Gabriel's retarded brother?"

"That he eats human flesh?" Sumner said. "I don't believe all of that talk. That's grammar-school gossip. Anyway, I don't care if he swallows snakes whole. Him and that swaggering brother of his are backshooters that couldn't flag down a gut-wagon before they started murdering people for fun and profit."

Garrett turned his back to the stove. He looked big and rugged, standing there warming his hands. He twitched the black mustache.

"Luther Gabriel is the most wanted man in the

territory, Sumner," he said. "He's a gun expert that always carries four or five on him. He's a tricky sonofabitch that never gives another man a fair fight. He'd just as soon shoot a baby in the head as wring a chicken's neck."

"I guess," Sumner said.

"He's killed three sheriffs, Sumner," Garrett went on. "That seems to be his favorite pastime. I know of a sheriff down south of here and at least one marshal that quit their jobs when they heard Gabriel was heading into their jurisdiction."

Sumner shook his handsome head. "That's what makes this profession seem worthwhile," he said sardonically.

Garrett grinned. "I know you ain't a world-saver," he said, "but maybe the money ain't worth it in this case. He's got that Billy Lobo with him now, and a Mexican named Cuesta. Cuesta killed his own mother, for God's sake."

"I have a separate dodger on him," Sumner said.

"Lobo is fast, maybe as fast as you," Garrett went on. "The rumor is, he made Bonney back down."

Garrett came over to Sumner. "Lobo wears his piece right here, across his thigh. It's a Joslyn .44, and it sits in a special holster that's greased up for fast action. They say you can't see his hand go to the gun."

Sumner smiled easily. "Would you quit wet-nursing me, old friend? This is my job, just like lawing is yours. It's the only thing I do well. People like Gabriel keep me in business, remember. Just like they do you. You and I would have to turn to cattle droving or clerking if nobody broke the law."

He was joking, but Garrett recognized the truth in it. Anyway, Sumner had pretty well proved he could take care of himself. He was not just blinding fast with a gun. He could put a hole in a silver dollar at fifty yards with a sidearm—and in a crosswind.

"That saloon is probably open," Garrett grinned. "Maybe I'll risk just one Red Top with you."

Sumner returned the grin. "Now that's the Pat Garrett we all know and admire," he said.

Chapter Two

Not far from Bernardo, in the black of a cold February night, five men waited for a train. It was just three days after Sumner had visited Pat Garrett in Lincoln, about a hundred miles to the southeast.

The temperature had dropped once again, and there had been a light, dry snowfall earlier in the day. It was the kind of night when cattlemen worried some about losing calves to the cold and when townsfolks huddled near their stoves and fireplaces, trying to keep warm. Snow squeaked underfoot in dark streets, and icicles hung along eaves in glistening rows, heavy and wintry looking.

The five mounted men huddled on their horses, beside a dead mesquite tree. They were gathered there just twenty feet from the railroad track which led into Bernardo only three miles distant. A Union Pacific local was due in fifteen minutes, and it was on time.

The men were the Gabriel brothers and their gang. Luther Gabriel had planned this train robbery for weeks, ever since he had verified through separate sources that this particular train would be carrying a silver shipment to Bernardo. If his facts were right, there would be silver dollars and bullion aboard, bound for the First Territorial Bank in Bernardo, and there would be enough of a haul in the robbery to last all of them quite some time, even split up five ways.

Luther Gabriel had a big reputation in the territory now, a reputation that stretched into Texas and Colorado. He did not always work with underlings, except for his retarded brother. But when he tackled a train, he usually liked to have several guns, because shipments of gold or silver ordinarily had guards aboard. So over the past several weeks, he had gathered three men to him, two he had ridden with before and one new face.

Luther Gabriel sat his mount uneasily, staring down the track. He was a big, bulky man with a full beard and dark, piercing eyes that seemed to bore right through a man to the very soul of him. His frosty breath fogged the night with regularity, and a light steam rose off him and his mount, a dark brown gelding. A thick scar cut across his left cheek, beginning just under his eye and running crosswise down almost to his mouth. It was the result of a knife fight in a Dodge City saloon years ago, before he had become the most feared outlaw in the territory. A drop of moisture hung under his nostrils, and he did not seem to notice. He glanced toward the smaller man mounted on a dun mare beside him, his brother Corey "Coot" Gabriel. Behind Coot, the three hirelings sat their mounts.

"What time is it?" Gabriel said in a deep, gruff voice, a voice that sounded like it had been dredged up from a rock quarry.

Coot gave his older brother a look and pulled a pocket watch out of his coat pocket. "It ain't quite time. There's still over five minutes." Like Luther Gabriel, this younger brother was dressed in a bear coat, so that he sat bulkily on his mount. He was a slight man in comparison to Luther, with a pale, rather ugly face, bland and often expressionless, with stringy hair that had an almost transparent look. He had never learned to read or write, and it had been an accomplishment to be able to tell time on his railroad watch. He had taken the watch from a conductor he had killed in a previous train holdup. He had ended the conductor's life quite unnecessarily by slicing the unfortunate man's throat from one ear to the other and then gutting him.

Those who had met up with the Gabriel brothers and survived to talk about it would never forget Coot. He had that vacant, unnerving look in his eyes that meant there was little human behind them. He carried hatchets and knives with him wherever he went and loved to cut flesh with them. He enjoyed slicing parts off of animals and humans alike, and then watching death come to his victims.

Behind Gabriel, a lean, sallow-faced man sat leaning on his saddlehorn. He was Billy Lobo, the gunslinger Garrett had mentioned to Sumner. He had killed a well-known gunfighter up in Montana, and nobody wanted to go against him. In his mid-twenties, Lobo was from a poor family in Texas and his only claim to skill was his fast draw. Gabriel had little respect for him, however, because Lobo knew nothing about the weapon with which he killed, and Gabriel prided himself on his knowledge of guns. Lobo had the cold blue stare of a wanton killer, and nobody wanted him around, not even other outlaws, except for Gabriel.

"It's coming," he said in a soft, whispery voice. "I can feel the ground move. Can't you?"

He was addressing Gabriel, but Gabriel did not reply. The train was still obviously miles away, and nobody but a crazy man would think he could feel the rumble of it in the ground at this distance. Gabriel did not reply to craziness.

"That's bullshit," the rider beside Lobo said. "Nobody can feel no goddam ground moving yet. That train is nowhere near yet."

He was a dope addict simply called Nightshade, because he was hooked on various forms of delusional narcotics, including the locally grown peyote. He was on a high at that moment, a look of foolish giddiness on his bizarre face, and it was only because his judgment was clouded that he dared contradict Lobo.

Lobo gave him a blistering look. "You couldn't feel the goddam train if it was running over your goddam chest," he offered in a hissing, sibilant voice.

Gabriel had hired Nightshade, though, because of his expertise in demolition. He had been in the War Between the States many years ago, as a kid, and had learned it there. A Confederate shell had

29

blown up near him at the end of that war and had destroyed part of his face; now he was a spectacle to behold. One eyeless socket was closed off with scar tissue. Only a part of his nose remained and a section of his jawbone was gone. He was in pain all the time, and that was why he had gotten onto the hallucinatory drugs. He scared people with his appearance, and grown men often crossed the street when they saw him coming.

Now the fifth man of the group spoke up, the one on the far side of Nightshade. "Why don't you two let it go?" he muttered in a Spanish accent. His name was Jesus Cuesta, and he was originally from Monterey. He had run into Gabriel not long ago in Albuquerque and had been looking for just such a project as this one. He had ridden with Gabriel once before, as had Nightshade. Cuesta had murdered his own mother in a fit of rage when in his teens and had been forced to leave Mexico because the Federales came after him. He was an old hand at train robbery and had no hesitation at all in killing anybody who could later identify him.

Nightshade turned his grotesque face toward Cuesta. His good eye was the color of slate, and it stared at Cuesta blankly now, expressionless, like a shark's eye. That was what Cuesta disliked most about Nightshade, you could not tell what was going on in his head by looking into his face. He had not liked it that Gabriel had hired Nightshade on again just to plant some dynamite and to have an extra gun. He liked to have people around him he could trust and understand. He got nothing from the addict beside him. He noticed Gabriel glance down the track now and followed Gabriel's stare. There was a sound coming out of the blackness.

"Listen!" Gabriel said through the heavy beard. They all turned now, and the sound was becoming more distinct. They could hear the faint chugging of the train's engine in the dark, and a slight rumble came from the tracks not far away.

"That's it!" Coot said loudly. Unlike his brother's voice, his was rather high and reedy, and a little childlike. "It's here!"

Gabriel turned toward Nightshade and jerked his head. Nightshade nodded and spurred his mount away from the others, down toward the track. He dismounted there, picketed the horse to a leafless bush hung with snow, and took a few steps down to a place near the rails of the track. There he glanced at Gabriel, got a nod from the big man, and took a match and lighted a fuse that led to the small packet of dynamite lying on the near rail. The fuse crackled and fizzed in the snow, but burned toward the explosives. Nightshade rose and got his mount and moved off away from the rail bed.

Now the train was in sight. A lone headlight shone toward them, cutting a bright hole in the darkness, and they could see the hulking shape of the black engine, chugging along like some prehistoric animal in the darkness. The train came on, getting bigger and bigger, and Gabriel glanced toward the fuse and dynamite. In the next instant, a violent, yellow explosion ripped the night,

31

smacking against their eardrums and making Coot Gabriel wince under its impact. Almost at the same instant, there was a screeching of brakes along the rails as the engineer tried to halt the lumbering mass of metal before it derailed. The train, only an engine, two freight cars, and a caboose, came grinding to a stop just short of the riders, making a big racket there, steam hissing and metal clanking.

"Let's go, boys!" Gabriel yelled.

They did not cover their faces. Gabriel disdained such safe measures. They rode on down to the train, yelling and whooping, their mounts kicking up snow and dirt. Coot and Lobo rode up on either side of the engine while Gabriel and Nightshade rode on down to the first freight car, the one where shards of amber light stabbed through cracks in the wooden sides. Cuesta rode on back to the caboose.

On Coot's side of the engine, the engineer came down off the engine with hands up, a bandannaed figure wearing a sheepskin coat and a scared look on his narrow face. Coot aimed a Wells Fargo revolver at him, a wild grin on his sallow face, and shot the man through the right eye. While the roar of his Wells Fargo revolver was still echoing in the cold stillness, spatterings of crimson and dull gray matter struck the greasy metal of the boiler behind the engineer, his one eye saucered in abject surprise. He then hit the hot metal hard, making a further red stain on its black surface, then slid to the rail underneath the wheels with the side of his head blown away.

The next couple of minutes were pure horror for those aboard the small train. While Gabriel and Nightshade shot the lock off the lighted baggage car, yelling for those inside to come out, Lobo was yanking a scared fireman off the tender on the far side of the engine.

"Don't shoot me. I got a wife and three kids to support!" the blocky, rather short fellow said into Lobo's face.

"Well, ain't that sweet," Lobo grated out in his sibilant whisper. "Is the little woman purty? Maybe it would be worth my time to go find her, too."

"I'm begging you," the fireman gushed in a short gasp.

Those were his last words. Lobo knocked him down with a blow to his head with the barrel of his Joslyn, dazing him. Then Lobo shoved the man's head and shoulders under the second wheel of the big engine. The fireman scrabbled to raise up, but could not. Lobo climbed up into the engine.

Meanwhile, Nightshade had slid the door of the baggage car open, and three men appeared with their hands up. They were marshal's deputies from down the line at Socorro. Gabriel's and Nightshade's guns blazed brightly, over and over again, and the three were torn up with hot lead. Down at the caboose, Cuesta had kicked in the front door and found a sleepy-eyed signalman there. The night was split once more with gunfire, and the signalman lay on the floor of the caboose, two bloody holes in his chest.

Gabriel was first aboard the baggage car, and he

saw the several bank bags immediately, lying on a big table in the center of the car. He and Nightshade opened them up and found just what Gabriel had expected, silver coins and bullion. But there wasn't nearly as much there as Gabriel had hoped.

The engine still chugged slowly up ahead as Gabriel stared at the gleaming silver.

"What's them bars worth?" Nightshade's grotesque face looked all twisted up in the yellow light.

"Not as much as I thought," Gabriel responded, more to himself than to his companion. "Them cheap sonsofbitches at the bank skimped on us. I wish they was in hell with their backs broke." He turned to Nightshade. "Remind me to kill me a banker the next time I see one."

Nightshade grinned.

"Let's get this stuff onto our mounts," Gabriel said.

It took only moments for him, Nightshade, and Cuesta to get the silver stuffed into saddlebags aboard their horses. Coot Gabriel had climbed aboard the engine with Lobo, and when he saw the fireman still under the wheel, regaining consciousness there, he looked into Lobo's face with a dull, vacant grin. "What you got in mind for that fellow?" He himself had just taken a razor-sharp bowie knife and amputated the ring finger of the engineer, just to get a gold wedding ring on the man's hand. The bloody finger now rested snugly in Coot's coat pocket, the ring still on it.

Lobo smiled an evil smile. He leaned out of the

cab and saw the other three mounted again and approaching the engine. Gabriel was in the lead. "Get mounted, Coot," Gabriel growled.

Coot never disobeyed his older brother. He jumped to the ground and walked to his mount, which was still nickering nervously from the shooting. He mounted up.

Gabriel handed Lobo a sack with silver in it. "It wasn't as much as we thought."

Lobo hefted the bag with a dour look on his thin, pale face. One never challenged Gabriel about the way he divvied up. A couple of men had and were now pushing up pansies in various cemeteries.

Gabriel turned to Cuesta and Nightshade, so they could hear him. "Like I said before, we'll split for a spell now, and then meet up again on the twentieth at Stinking Creek." There was a saloon whore there that had captured Gabriel's fancy the last time through. "Any questions?"

"Let's ride," Cuesta said in his accent.

Gabriel nodded. "Now send their train on in to them," he said to Lobo.

Lobo grinned and pulled on a lever, and the train started up. Coot remembered the fireman, and his face lit up dully. Down on the ground on the far side of the train, the fireman was just coming around sufficiently to see where he was. The big rear wheel of the engine began rolling toward his chest. He lifted and rolled just as the massive chunk of iron arrived, but did not get his right arm clear. The wheel rolled over it just below the shoulder, and neatly amputated it. The fireman yelled loudly, then collapsed beside the moving train, his good hand reaching spasmodically for the bloody stump.

Lobo had jumped off the train just in time to see it, and was considerably disappointed that the unfortunate man had not been cut in half. His hand went to his gun to finish the fellow off, but then he decided against it. This was just as good.

The train had clack-clacked past now, and Coot gave Lobo a hard grin from across the undamaged tracks. He thought of taking the severed arm with him, but then Lobo was riding off to join the others, and Coot followed. Down the line, in the cold blackness of the night, the train had almost reached Bernardo.

It was just a couple of days later that O'Brien arrived in Stinking Creek to visit Aaron Seger.

O'Brien had not seen Seger in years and was looking forward to this break in hunting to catch up on old times with one of the few men O'Brien considered a friend. Seger and O'Brien both came from eastern Tennessee, in the hills, and Seger had been a friend of the family until moving west. O'Brien had come on him quite by accident, not long after O'Brien had taken up buffalo hunting as a profession, and they had done some drinking together, remembering the hard days in Tennessee. Seger had been married then with a six-year-old daughter, but his wife had died since with the scarlet fever. When O'Brien's own family had been

36

taken off with influenza not long afterward, Seger had gotten the news before O'Brien and had had to tell O'Brien of the tragedy the next time O'Brien came past.

Now Seger's daughter was standing on the threshold of puberty, and the first thing O'Brien learned upon his arrival in Stinking Creek was that Annie Seger would be confirmed in the local Catholic church the very next day. O'Brien was glad he had arrived at such an auspicious moment in their lives and attended the confirmation with Seger and Annie and some of Seger's local friends.

It was a sunny morning at the church, and the temperature had risen. The women attending had little edges of mud on the hems of their long, pretty dresses. There was a lot of ritual in Latin that O'Brien did not understand, a lot of white satin and lace, and a quiet solemnity that reminded O'Brien of the way it was before a hunt. O'Brien stood in his rawhides at the back of the church and took pleasure in Seger's pleasure. When it was over, the three of them returned to Seger's quarters behind the local railway express station. Seger was the local agent for the Union Pacific and had been for many years.

Seger and O'Brien sat down in Seger's parlor where Seger used to sit with his wife when she was alive, and Annie made them some coffee. The room was rather spartan, an old sofa along one wall, some straight chairs sitting about, and a china cupboard near the door. Hooked rugs decorated a wood plank floor, and there were white curtains at a couple of windows that Annie kept clean, but the place lacked a mature woman's touch.

"Yeah, I'm real proud of Annie," Seger was saying as they relaxed at the table in the center of the room. Annie was heard in the kitchen, getting their coffee ready. She loved to fuss for visitors, and O'Brien was a special one.

"You have every right to be, Aaron," O'Brien told him. "You raised her real good. Just like Abby would like it."

Seger smiled. He was a few years O'Brien's senior, a heavyset fellow with thinning brown hair and the beginning of a paunch at his belt. He wore a plaid shirt and dungarees, even though he had just attended a very formal church ceremony. "Well, I done as good as I could," he said. "Annie ain't needed much guidance. She's just as level-headed and smart as her mother."

"You always provided for your kin good," O'Brien said. "That says a lot for a man." He lay back on his chair. "And you saw that Annie got her schooling."

"Some of it was hard," Seger admitted. There had been a time after his wife's death when he had felt as if he were sitting in the wreckage of a violent storm, and although he had survived its ferocity, he might never be a whole man again. "How's it been with you, O'Brien? The shaggies keeping you in grub?"

O'Brien nodded. "So far, Aaron. But it's thinning out. Buffalo bones are beginning to whiten the plains out there. Ranchers are collecting them and selling them to fertilizer makers. The best days are gone."

Seger started to reply, but Annie came into the room carrying a tray with coffee on it. "I hope you like this coffee, O'Brien," she said in a rather high but melodic voice. "It's a new brand we got here now. Comes up from Colombia, they say."

"Ain't she a whiz?" Seger grinned.

Annie put the tray down and placed two big steaming cups of coffee before the men. She was a rather tall girl for her age, just breaking into womanhood, with small breasts showing. She had long, blondish hair like her mother had had and very light blue eyes. She was not really pretty, but other women were beginning to call her handsome. She was a bright, sensitive girl, though, even more so than her father knew. "You said you'd show me the buffalo robe you brought us," she said to O'Brien. When she was younger, she had always been a little frightened by O'Brien's appearance, but now she had a small crush on him.

"Not just now, honey," Seger told her. "We want to talk some man talk for a spell. He'll bring the robe in after our coffee."

Annie pulled a face, making O'Brien smile. "Oh, okay," she said reluctantly.

"We'll see how it fits in your room," O'Brien said.

Annie had hoped he would say that. "I shall have an awful time waiting," she smiled.

She disappeared into the kitchen again, and O'Brien shook his shaggy head and ran fingers across his dark brown mustache. "That's one fine girl, Aaron."

Seger nodded his agreement. "That's why I'm trying to decide on what to do next," he said.

O'Brien furrowed his dark brow. "What do you mean?"

Seger sighed. "This territory's gone to hell in a basket the last few years. Bad men are coming in faster than the law can handle them. You hear about the train robbery the other day, near Bernardo?"

O'Brien shook his head. "Can't say I did."

"Six trainmen killed." He glanced toward the kitchen and lowered his voice. "Butchered, I hear. The rumor is, it's the Gabriel gang."

"Never heard of them," O'Brien said.

Seger grunted. "You will. They're just plain murderers, O'Brien."

O'Brien had a Christian name, a rather Biblical one, that Seger knew well, but ever since O'Brien's father had died, O'Brien had been called simply by his family name. Nobody in the territory knew his first name, except for Seger and Annie.

"I've ran into a few like that," O'Brien said. "But what does that got to do with you and Annie?"

Seger shrugged. "Some express stations been hit, too. Not close by, but it makes you think. Hell, it's just a gut feeling I got, that maybe we outlasted our welcome around here. This ain't no fit place for a young lady, O'Brien, and that's what Annie will be one day soon."

O'Brien nodded. "You got a point," he said. He

would hate to see Seger go. It had been nice thinking he was out there, a friend from back home, even though O'Brien rarely saw him. But Seger was right. The West was no place for a young woman of marriageable age, and that was what Annie would be in a few years. "Where would you go?"

Seger hunched his heavy shoulders. "Hell, I don't know. Not back to Tennessee. Maybe just to St. Louis, where I could get her into a good school. I hear there are railroad jobs there."

O'Brien was pensive. "You might be better off."

Seger decided to change the subject. "You going to hang your hat here for a few days? It sure would be good to jaw with you a while, pardner."

O'Brien smiled. "I'll stay tonight, Aaron. But I can't afford any long off time. I got to keep hunting this winter. And with McGraw laid up, I'm on my own again. That's really the best way, when you get right to it, but it takes more of your time."

"You always was a loner," Seger commented. "I guess you always will be. Just like your old daddy."

O'Brien rose from his chair. "Let's go break out that robe for Annie," he said.

"She'll like that," Seger told him.

A few moments later they were outside in the warming sun, untying the dark buffalo robe from O'Brien's Appaloosa's saddle.

By noon that day, the snow was melting fast, and icicles were dripping along eaves on buildings in Stinking Creek and all through that part of the territory. Over in Bernardo, Certainty Sumner rode into town just after noon and hitched his black stallion to the rail outside the Pot of Gold Saloon and went inside for a drink and eats.

It was a quiet morning. There were four men standing at the bar inside, and one was seated at a table, drinking by himself. A blocky bartender wiped at the countertop with a cloth as the four men spoke together in low tones.

The Pot of Gold was not a fancy place. The floor was wood planks dusted with sawdust, and there were hand-rived timbers supporting a roof overhead. Behind the bar on the wall was a large mirror that had the silvering flaking off its backside. Rows of bottles sat on shelves on either side of the mirror. The bartender glanced at the newcomer, then took a second look. He had worked in a saloon in Alburquerque a year ago and had had Sumner pointed out to him. And when a man had Sumner pointed out to him, he never forgot it.

"Well, I'll be damned," he said softly.

Sumner gave him a somber look. He did not like to be recognized. You did not call out a man's name in the West to identify him to others, but some fools forgot that unwritten rule. Sumner hoped this man was not one of them.

"Pour me a glass of that B and B whiskey," Sumner said in his modulated, educated-sounding voice. His acquline face had a light patina of dust on it, and when he took his dark hat off, there was a line just above his brow where the clean flesh started. He adjusted the hat and replaced it over dark hair. His dark brown eyes glanced toward the four men, who looked like drifters to him. "And some boiled eggs and cheese would taste good, if you've got them back there."

The drifter nearest Sumner was a thick-set, brawny man wearing dusty trail clothes and a crumpled Stetson. He was studying Sumner closely, a half-sneer on his heavy features. He looked at Sumner's dark riding coat, which Sumner was now removing, and then saw the neat corduroy undercoat that was worn over a red vest. Sumner's trousers were corduroy too, tucked into black boots. His shirt under the vest was dark blue, and there was the blue cravat at his throat.

"Sonofabitch," the thick-set man muttered. He looked toward his comrades. "You ever see anything like this?"

The third man down the line stepped out from the bar to look at Sumner. He was slim with a hawk nose. He wore two pearl-handled revolvers that hung very low on him. "Shit," he commented.

The other two were staring now, too. One was taller than the others with the sourest face Sumner had ever seen. The one closest to the brawny one was a bit shorter than the brawny man, and looked like he could be related. "What we got ourselves here," he said jovially, "a goddam dandy?"

The tall man grunted. "Looks like a gambler to me. I hate gamblers."

Sumner glanced over toward them. He had seen their kind before. None of them would harass him if alone, but together they were like a pack of wolves.

"You a gambler, dude?" the brawny man asked Sumner.

Sumner ignored the question and reminded himself that there were men like this all over the territory, and a person had to avoid and ignore them whenever he could. It was people like this that had proved to Sumner long ago that it was not the strong who survive and replenish themselves in the world. Darwin's "fittest" were not the individuals with true strength. The strong made their stand against the world, not concerning themselves with consequences. They were eventually crushed by opposing forces because they would not bend to them. The weak, on the other hand, and the evil skulked about and avoided real trouble and only attacked when there was no big risk to themselves, like these men, and they survived and adapted. They molded themselves to the shape of the world, thinking always of protecting themselves at the expense of others. In the end, it was they who survived, along with cockroaches and scorpions.

"I asked you a question," the brawny man growled.

Now the tall man had separated himself from the bar, too. It was obvious they figured they had found themselves a diversion on a dull day.

The bartender suddenly looked nervous. "Gentlemen, there's something you ought to know before you—"

"Shut your mouth!" the short man beside the big one said in a harsh tone. "Just keep out of it!"

The bartender swallowed his tension. Over at

44

the table, the other customer slowly rose from his chair and moved out of the place, leaving a full glass of whiskey behind, already paid for. The tall drifter glanced toward the table, saw the shot glass, and grinned. He walked easily over to the table across the room. He sat down facing Sumner, picked up the abandoned whiskey, and downed it in one gulp, never taking his hard eyes off the bounty hunter.

Sumner shook his head slightly, making a face. He always tried to avoid pointless trouble. "No," he said in a quiet, even voice, "I'm not a gambler." He glanced toward the bartender. "You getting that order or not?"

"He ain't getting it," the brawny drifter said, the closest one to Sumner.

"That's right," the shorter, younger one chimed in. He was just a kid, but Sumner knew kids could be dangerous. The kid giggled slightly and turned away, walking to the far end of the bar. There he turned the corner, went behind the bar, and came back toward them. The bartender looked frightened. "You're only serving us, barkeep. And I want something worth drinking."

The bartender backed away while the young drifter turned to the bottle shelf and looked through some labels. Strawlike yellowish hair stuck out from under a slouched hat, and he still had a pimpled lower face. He took a tall bottle from the shelf and turned back to the others. Because of his movement and also the tall drifter's, Sumner now found himself flanked by the group.

The kid took a short swig from the bottle, then

45

cracked the glass quart against the side of the bar. The broken bottle in his hand, he said flatly, "You might as well get, dandy. You ain't getting no liquor here."

"We don't want no goddam New Orleans types stinking up this place with their stinking perfumed hankies," the slim drifter down the bar said. He was facing Sumner now, whereas the brawny one nearest was still leaning on the bar. "This is a place for real men. Ain't that right, barkeep?"

The bartender just stood there, too scared to speak now. Sumner sighed. He could just leave, but that idea rankled him. The trouble was, too, that these men held no professional interest for him, since it was unlikely they had bounties on their heads.

"I've never worn perfume, but you smell like you might do with a splash of some. You smell and look like horse dung."

The slim man's face changed and revealed disbelief. Then it clouded over like a rocky mesa under thunderheads. The brawny man turned slowly toward Sumner and squared off with him. Sumner ignored it all and spoke again to the bartender. "Bring that stuff over to this table," he gestured, "and don't make me wait all day."

Sumner turned and headed for a table between the one where the tall drifter now sat and the door to the outside. Halfway there, he was stopped by the hard voice of the big brawny man.

"Where the hell you think you're going, lily-liver?"

Sumner stopped and turned a quarter turn. He

wasn't flanked as badly now, but they presented a loose semicircle to him at various distances. The tall drifter at the table was now the closest, and his hands were not in view.

"Why don't you let it go?" Sumner said softly.

"You heard what he said," the slim, narrow-faced drifter said to his partner, from beyond the brawny one. "He's mine."

Sumner carefully shoved his coattails back out of his way and exposed the deadly looking Peacemaker on his gunbelt. The long revolver hung on a slant across his waist, out in front of him, slung across his belly. It was the first thing you saw when he opened up the coat. The bottom of the holster was strapped to his left thigh, and the bone handle pointed at his right hand.

"There's plenty for both of us," the brawny man growled.

"I'm going to blow your liver right out of your back," the slim fellow breathed. "I'm going to cut you to pieces, dandy."

"You going to do it—or just talk about it?" Sumner said in a suddenly low, hard voice.

In the next instant, the slim drifter went for the revolver hanging low on his hip. The brawny man started a draw just a split second later.

It was then that Certainty Sumner exploded into movement, a movement that was too fast for the eye to follow. His hand went to the Peacemaker magically, and the gun appeared in it as if it had been there all the time. The Colt began firing in staccato fashion as he fanned the hammer, dropping into a half crouch at the same moment.

47

Sumner's eye told him that even though the slim man had drawn first, the brawny one was faster, so that drifter was his first target.

Sumner's revolver erupted loudly in the room, interspersed with other gunshots, and it all occurred in the space of seconds with Sumner fanning the gun and reaiming. His first shot beat the brawny man by a mile and hit him directly over the heart, exploding it like a paper bag and sending the big fellow crashing against the bar. The big man's gun went off then, firing into the floor at Sumner's feet. Sumner's second shot hit the slim drifter in the forehead, traveled through his skull like a hot poker, and blew the crown of his head off. He had aimed and fired at Sumner, but the shot only tore at Sumner's coatsleeve, then smashed an oil lamp hanging on a hook in the far corner. Sumner had seen movement under the table where the tall man sat, and his third shot went off simultaneously with the seated man's. He felt hot lead graze his side under the coat, and then his third and fourth shots hit the tall man in the low chest and neck. Just as the young fellow behind the bar was drawing, Sumner turned and blew the gun out of his hand with a fifth shot, cracking bones in the fingers, and then smashing two bottles over the kid's head with the last shot, making liquor cascade down all over the kid's head and face.

Now the brawny drifter finally hit the floor at the bar, and the slim one took a far table down with him as he crashed across it, splintering wood and making a big racket. His legs kicked at the floor for a moment, but he had been dead when the bullet entered his brain. The tall drifter had been blown backwards on his chair and now lay jerking for a moment at the far wall, finally motionless. The kid behind the bar was holding his destroyed hand and staring wide-eyed toward Sumner.

Acrid-smelling, bitter-tasting gunsmoke filled the now-quiet room, but the bartender's ears were still ringing with the din. He looked around the room at the three bloody corpses and then glanced at the scared kid with the sticky liquor and busted glass all over him. Sumner had risen from his crouch. He twirled the Peacemaker backward three times in a fluid, easy movement, then it came forward one turn and nestled softly into its holster.

"Sonofabitch," the bartender muttered thickly. He had never seen anything like that in his entire life. *"Sonofabitch!"*

'I don't think I like the calibre of your customers," Sumner said in the smooth voice. "Cancel that order. I'll eat across the street."

A moment later he strode easily through the slatted doors, looking as relaxed as when he had come in.

The bartender just stared after him. A few feet away, the kid had begun to tremble all over.

Chapter Three

Sumner learned very little about the Gabriel gang in Bernardo, except how they had murdered everyone aboard the train they had robbed just outside of town. When Sumner learned how they had mauled the fireman, under the wheels of the engine, he just shook his head slowly. That was typical of the Gabriels and the men with which they rode.

A local marshal came to question Sumner about the shootings at the saloon, but when he got the whole story from the bartender, he left Sumner alone and with great relief. The kid Sumner had left alive had ridden out without getting any medical help for the busted hand. He did not want to be around to confront Sumner again. On Sumner's second day in Bernardo, when he was just finishing a midday meal at the local café, a boy about the age of puberty came in and approached Sumner's table. The apron-decorated proprietor, standing across the sunlit room, scowled at the boy, but the boy ignored him.

"You Certainty Sumner?" the boy asked Sumner.

Sumner looked up from his plate, chewing.

"I just wanted to shake your hand," the boy said.

"Get out of here, kid," Sumner told him, wiping at his mouth with a napkin.

"I seen Jesse James," the boy persisted.

Sumner looked over at him and shook his head.

"He come through here a couple months ago. Called hisself Mr. Howard. You can ask the marshal. The marshal, he kept out of Jesse's way."

Sumner regarded the boy soberly.

"Jesse let me shake his hand," the kid said.

Sumner smiled slightly. "You think Mr. James is some kind of hero, kid?" Sumner knew the reward on Jesse was high, but the James gang almost never operated in the territory Sumner was working.

The boy shrugged. "I don't know. Some say he is."

"He and Frank are cold-blooded killers, boy," Sumner said more slowly and seriously. "Don't believe everything you hear." He stuck his hand out. The boy's eyes brightened, and he grabbed Sumner's hand in a frail one, and Sumner shook it.

"Now get," Sumner said.

"You been asking about them Gabriel men," the boy said, standing his ground.

Sumner sighed heavily. "So?"

"I heard a drifter talking after the robbery. He said Luther Gabriel used to hang out sometimes in Stinking Creek."

Sumner's dark eyes narrowed down. "Who was the drifter?"

"I don't know," the boy answered. "But he sounded positive about it. He talked about the gang some more, too. Said that a couple of them was seen over in Willard a while back and that they might go back there."

"Did he tell your marshal any of that?"

"I don't think so," the boy said. "He was just passing through, drinking over at the saloon."

Sumner thought about all of that for a moment, the reached into a pocket and pulled out a silver coin. He held it out, and the boy took it. "There. That's for your trouble."

The boy's eyes had widened. "Gosh. Thanks, Sumner."

"Now let me finish my meal in peace," Sumner told him, picking up a wine glass.

"You bet," the boy said. "I'm pleasured to meet you, Sumner."

A moment later the boy was gone. Sumner, sitting there pensively, realized that one never knew from where information would come. He believed the kid, and he sure had nothing to lose by riding over to Willard to check the town out.

He put his napkin down and rose from the table. "I'll take the bill now," he said to the proprietor. "I've been in Bernardo long enough, it seems. People are beginning to call me by name."

About a hundred miles west of Bernardo, on that same day, O'Brien was out hunting again. There wasn't as much snow now, but tracking was tougher, and even the small herds of shaggies were hard to find. He kind of missed McGraw, too, because he had become accustomed to the presence of the rough-hewn hunter in hardship camp. Now that McGraw was up some in age, he was getting as untrustworthy as a Kansas City lawyer, but his gruff voice and rude manner went down well with O'Brien. His appearance would scare crows out of a cornfield, and sometimes O'Brien thought that if McGraw's brains were dynamite, the fellow couldn't blow the top of his head off. But he did know buffalo, and he would never steal from another man's saddle wallet.

On this frosty morning, at almost midday, O'Brien finally found a group of five shaggies huddled under a bone-bare stand of cottonwood in rather hilly country. They must have gotten separated from a larger herd, he figured. Four of the five were scrawny, ugly animals, but the fifth had a dark reddish robe of good quality. It was a big bull with good horns and long legs. O'Brien had left the Appaloosa down the break and was coming up on them in a crosswind. They were still five hundred yards off and seemed skittery, so O'Brien knew he had to make the kill at a distance. He moved up toward them a bit more, keeping his body hidden as well as he could by some dead undergrowth that stuck up out of the melting snow. He had the Sharps rifle with him, the big gun that could fire accurately at a half-mile and knock a target down at any distance it could reach.

He came up to the edge of the undergrowth and set up a tripod that came with the gun, and then mounted the rifle on the tripod. His hands began to ache from the cold, and his breath came out in white wisps. He pulled the big sight up on the rifle and got down on his belly and sighted through it. There was his target, not looking very big at that distance. O'Brien settled against the big gun and put his finger on the trigger. He hesitated, wrinkling his nose. He thought he had scented something in the cold air, something other than buffalo. But now the smell was gone. He aimed again carefully and squeezed the trigger.

The long gun erupted explosively, kicking back against O'Brien's big, muscular shoulder. Five hundred yards away, the buffalo dropped like a stone.

The other animals bolted, running off. But O'Brien did not want any of them, anyway. He got up and squinted toward the kill. The buffalo was lifeless. O'Brien rarely missed a shot, either be it from a stationary position or galloping into a herd full tilt, firing as he rode. McGraw considered him the best shot in the business.

O'Brien left the rifle where it stood on its tripod and started out toward the dark hulk in the snow. He was almost to the animal when he got the other scent again, and strong. At almost the same instant, the wolves appeared over a nearby rise of ground.

There were five of them. They were big gray timber wolves, their narrow eyes staring at him and the dead bull. They looked lean and hungry.

"Oh, hell," O'Brien muttered.

He moved on up toward the dead shaggy, and the wolves just watched him from a small distance.

54

Then he heard the foremost of them growl deeply.

"You can't have it!" O'Brien yelled toward them. Two of them licked their chops, and one whined softly in the silence of the winter morning.

O'Brien had known a hunter who had been caught out alone by wolves. The fellow had shot his ammunition out, and then they had come in on him, tearing him to pieces. When he was found later, there were only his head, part of his torso, and his feet. The wolves had consumed the rest.

That was why O'Brien knew now, standing there confronting these animals, that they were not just interested in the buffalo. They wanted him, too. At that moment, he wished he had heeded his earlier warning and kept the Sharps with him. He would have settled now for just the Winchester on his mount's irons. But all he had was the .38 caliber Dardick 1500 revolver that hung on a gunbelt under his heavy clothing, which he sometimes wore to put a bullet into the brain of an animal if the first shot did not kill it. He got under his bearskin coat and grabbed at the handgun just as the wolves broke apart and came in toward him and the buffalo, growling deeply as they came, ears laid back.

"Get out of here!" O'Brien yelled, waving the gun.

They were not impressed. They came on down around him, ignoring the buffalo. O'Brien knew he could not wait. He aimed at the nearest wolf and shot it in the head. The animal jumped into the air spasmodically and then began kicking about in the snow. In the next instant, a second wolf jumped at O'Brien from a blind side.

O'Brien turned and shot in one movement as the weight of the animal knocked him down. The first shot just grazed the wolf, then O'Brien was on his back, and there was a lot of snarling in his face. His left hand was bitten as he tried to hold the animal off, the stink of it strong in his nostrils, the wild eyes crazy with hunger. Another wolf was on him now, tearing at his rawhide trousers. O'Brien pulled off a second and third round, and the wolf on his upper body fell away, yelping and kicking. The other one backed off at the shots with a piece of rawhide in its mouth. O'Brien fired off another shot and just grazed the animal as it moved about.

O'Brien rose to his knee. "Get away, you demons from hell!" he yelled loudly.

There were still three of them, and he was running out of ammunition. He did not figure they would give him time to reload if he stayed put. He got to his feet, aiming the revolver at the nearest one. The three now hung back, seeing the two dead animals of their pack. O'Brien started backing up in the direction he had come. One of them came at him, and he shouted again. It hesitated.

O'Brien kept backing away, stumbling, and finally had put twenty yards between them and him. One of them was already smelling at the corpse of the buffalo and had given up on O'Brien. he continued backing, and then all the wolves were on the carcass.

O'Brien stood back away from them. "All right, you bastards, take it!" he muttered. They were already tearing at it, destroying the hide he had wanted.

He kept backing away, and they would look up at him from time to time, but they were satisfied with the buffalo now. Finally he was able to turn away from them and trudge back to his rifle. When he got there, he turned to see if he could pick them off from there. But he realized they had ruined a lot of the hide by now, anyway, and they were difficult targets from here, eating at the buffalo from its far side.

"Sonofabitch," O'Brien muttered, watching them feed for a long moment. Then he picked up his gear, including the long rifle, and headed slowly back toward his horse.

It was a bad winter for hunting. He should probably just give it up for a few weeks, he thought. Aaron Seger had begged him to stick around for a while with free grub and lodging. O'Brien wished now he had. Well, he had heard there was a small herd over near Willard. He would try there. Pretty soon there would be a big thaw and the hunting would get better.

It was something to hope for.

Certainty Sumner arrived in Willard a few days later in the first week of March.

There was no law in Willard. There had been a sheriff for a while, a couple of years ago, and Luther Gabriel had killed him on a trip through there. Nobody had wanted to take the badge up then, after that killing.

Sumner made a stop at the local saloon, following up a hunch that the boy in Bernardo might have had correct information about part of the Gabriel gang. It was late afternoon when he walked into the place, and there were no other customers about.

It was a fancier place than the one where he had been challenged by the drifters in Bernardo. There was a painting of a reclining nude woman behind the long bar, and at the rear of the room there was a pocket billiards table. A dapper bartender stood behind the bar, wiping at a glass with a cloth. He wore a stiff collar and tie, and had a short handlebar mustache that curled up at the ends and was waxed to hold its shape. There was a faro table over on the wall across from the bar. A sign above it said, "Beat the Tiger." This was the kind of place that offered hot baths for a dollar out back and "soiled dove" in a frilly bedroom upstairs.

"Make it a shot of Planter's, barman," Sumner said in the smooth voice.

"Yessir," the bartender said rather formally. He got the liquor and poured Sumner a shot, and Sumner put a silver coin onto the bar. "Just passing through, mister?" He was eyeing Sumner's neat clothing.

Sumner did not touch the drink, nor did he respond to the question. "I'm here looking for some men," he said.

The bartender's eyebrows arched upward. He spilled some tobacco makings into a small white paper and tapered up a cigarette. He struck a long match and lighted it, and then puffed on it to get it going while Sumner waited patiently.

"A lot of people pass through here," the bartender finally said.

"These are known as the Gabriel gang," Sumner said to him. The rye was still untouched on the bar.

The bartender's eyes squinted down some, and Sumner could see fear creep into them. He looked at Sumner differently. "Are you . . . part of that outfit?"

Sumner gave him a look. "I didn't think it was courtesy to ask a man's business."

The bartender looked more frightened than ever. This handsome, well-attired stranger didn't look the type to ride with the likes of Luther Gabriel, but you couldn't be sure of such things. "I didn't mean to put forward a saucy manner," he apologized quickly. "Fact is, there was some of Gabriel's men in here—and just last night."

A kind of hard tranquility settled deep into Sumner's gut. "You know which ones they were?" He took a gold coin from a pocket and laid it on the bar.

The bartender nodded and seemed to relax some.

"There was three of them, and I recognized two. One was that Billy Lobo, the gunfighter. When he come in, most of my other customers left."

Sumner picked up the rye and swigged it down in one gulp. "Go on."

"Then there was that one called Nightshade. He come in later with this third man, a Mexican. You never seen a face like the one on that Nightshade.

59

He scared off the rest of my regulars."

"I've heard about his face," Sumner said.

"Hearing ain't seeing," the bartender offered, opening up some now, realizing Sumner was not one of them. "I heard a couple of cowpokes talking about him, later, after they were gone. Seems he knows dynamite, and that's the only reason anybody will keep him around. They needed him to stop that train at Bernardo. He chews peyote."

"Sounds like a real nice fellow," Sumner put in.

The other man nodded wryly. "These cowpokes said Nightshade hunted buffalo for a while. The word is he could spook a herd by just showing himself. He's the one that had the run-in with that hunter called O'Brien."

Sumner frowned quizzically. "O'Brien?"

The bartender laughed in his throat. "I thought everybody in this territory had heard of that one. He's a mountain man, one of them buffalo hunters that's more animal than human. This Nightshade come into a saloon one night in Abilene with another hunter—this was years ago. They found this O'Brien in there and this other hunter, a fellow named Mule Something-or-other, began hoorawing O'Brien. A big ruckus started between them with Mule putting two bullets into O'Brien, who was unarmed. But O'Brien come in on him right through the lead, grabbed the hunter's hand that held the gun, and squeezed. He busted every bone in that man's hand, and then he proceeded to beat him to death. It was like a brown bear had gone crazy. Nightshade tried to shoot him then, but his rifle misfired. O'Brien tore the rifle from

60

him and swung it against his head. Nightshade went down like a sack of grain, and O'Brien must have thought he was dead. He finally calmed down then, but the owner of the saloon says he busted both of his swinging doors when he banged out of the place."

Sumner made a soft sound in his throat. "This O'Brien sounds like my kind of man," he said quietly. "Too bad he didn't finish Nightshade off."

"I doubt you'd like him if you met him," the bartender said. "He came in here last fall. A store across the street closed up till he left. He came in here looking seven feet tall, his rawhides stinking of buffalo, and laid that Winchester of his down on my bar. He don't go unarmed anymore. He ordered whiskey and I give him a half-full bottle. He drank it without taking the bottle from his lips, honest to God. You never heard of him, huh?"

Sumner sighed. He had let the barkeep talk to loosen him up. "Let's get back to Gabriel's men. Did the three of them leave together?"

The other man nodded. "Late last night about midnight. They was in here two nights ago, too. I think they're staying just outside of town somewhere. They rode off to the east, so they might be out at that old Thurmond shack to save hotel expenses. It's been abandoned for some time."

Sumner nodded and laid another gold coin on the bar. He leaned forward slightly toward the bartender. "We never had this little talk. I never came in here. You understand me?"

The cigarette in the bartender's right hand

61

dropped some ashes onto the mahogany bar and he brushed at them. He nodded. "Yes."

Sumner left the saloon then, and it was getting dark outside. He took a long riding coat off and packed it into his saddlebag. It was a reasonably warm night for March, and he did not want to be encumbered for what he was about to do. He still wore the curduroy undercoat. He took the Colt .45 from its holster, checked its ammunition, and reholstered it. Then he removed the Colt Model .41 derringer from a smaller holster at the middle of his back at the waist and made sure it also was loaded. A moment later he was aboard the black stallion and heading out to the east of town to find the cabin mentioned by the bartender.

It was dark by the time he saw the lighted shack off to the east, not far from the stage track. The small structure glowed warmly in the night, surrounded by patchy snow. There was a hitching rail out back, and Sumner saw mounts tethered back there.

He dismounted a hundred yards from the place and shoved a picket stake into the soft ground, picketing the stallion there. Then he approached the cabin on foot.

He arrived there just moments later and moved quietly up to a window on the south side of the place. He carefully removed the Peacemaker from its resting place and went up close to the window. Part of it was busted, and inside there was a thin swatch of burlap to keep the cold out. The burlap hung crookedly, though, and left a corner open through which one could see into the interior.

Sumner bent down to take a look and heard something behind him. He whirled quickly, and all he saw was a club descending from above. He raised the Peacemaker to fire, but in the next instant the club cracked into the side of his face. Bright lights exploded inside his head and then went out completely.

It seemed like only a moment later that Sumner regained consciousness when the ice cold water was thrown onto him. He came to quickly, and the first thing he felt through the cold of the water was the stabbing pain throbbing in his face and head. Blood had run down from the wound near his temple and had stained his cravat, shirt, and coat. He shook his head, and it hurt even more. He looked around and saw the three men through blurred vision. He was tied to one of the two interior posts that held the roof of the cabin up, and he was slumped but in a standing position.

"Well, well," the lean, sallow-faced man in front of him said in a sibilant whisper. It was Billy Lobo, and he had an ugly grin on his narrow face. "The dude is alive after all."

Another voice, Spanish-accented, came from behind him. "I did not hit him hard. I could have killed him with that pick handle."

Sumner focused on them. The swarthy man just behind Lobo had to be the Mexican, the one called Cuesta. He turned slightly and saw the third face, and it was a sight to behold. It was the face of Nightshade, and Sumner had never seen it before.

The half nose, the scar tissue, the one shark eye, all combined frighteningly.

"Look what I found in his pockets," Nightshade said. His voice was low and tough sounding. He was dead sober because he had not been able to find any drugs to keep him satisfied. But just a few days ago, on their way here, he had raped and murdered a fifteen-year-old girl they had found alone on a farm, while still under the influence of peyote.

Lobo took the paper from Nightshade and glanced at it. It was a wanted poster on Luther Gabriel. He looked up somberly from the paper into Sumner's face. "Well, I'll be a sonofabitch. This here is a bounty hunter, I'd bet my mount on it."

Sumner returned Lobo's hard stare. Things were coming into focus for him. He knew that Lobo was considered lightning fast with a gun and a deadly killer. He was very angry with himself. Cuesta must have been outside when Sumner approached, probably back tending the horses. He had undoubtedly just stumbled onto Sumner by accident. Sumner had been so intent on seeing inside, he had let Cuesta surprise him. It was the only time that had happened to him since he had taken up bounty hunting.

"Who are you, mister?" Cuesta said harshly. He came and grabbed Sumner by the hair and shook his head. "Are you after us for goddam bounties?"

Sumner knew that outlaws hated bounty hunters even more than lawmen. He just stared back at them.

"You answer us, you bastard," Lobo said, drawing his Joslyn .44 revolver and sticking the muzzle up under Sumner's chin, "or I'll blow the top of your goddam head off."

Sumner looked into those hostile faces and figured it was all over for him finally. In his line of work, your luck could run out fast—and his had. No matter how careful a man was, there were moments when his guard was down. Then hell could descend in an instant, exploding your world into eternity.

"Why don't you stuff it up your ass," he growled.

Lobo's face went wild, and his finger tightened over the trigger of the Joslyn. But then Nightshade intervened. He grabbed Lobo's hand. "Wait a minute," he said. "Maybe this will work."

He had picked up the pick handle with which Cuesta had hit Sumner. Now Cuesta and Lobo moved away from Sumner as Nightshade came before him with the hardwood club. He grinned evilly through his half face and swung the club at Sumner.

It hit him hard in the ribs, cracking one audibly. He yelled aloud in pain as the hurt rocketed through his torso, then he slumped even farther on the post, his breath coming hard and irregular.

Nightshade grinned and swung the club again and again. It hit Sumner in the left arm and then the head. He thought he felt the arm break. Bright lights cascaded through his skull again, and he went out for the second time.

"For Christ's sake, you overdid it," Cuesta complained.

"I'll just put a bullet in his brain," Lobo said.

"Hell, why not?" Cuesta put in. "He was probably alone, anyway. I'm getting thirsty and ready to go into town."

Lobo put the gun to Sumner's head for the second time. Again Nightshade spoke up. "Let me have him. I'll do it my own way." He grinned malevolently. "Then I'll join you later in town."

Lobo lowered the revolver. "Oh, shit. You can have him."

He holstered the gun, and a moment later he and Cuesta left, riding off to town. Nightshade went and got more cold water and threw it onto Sumner's hanging head. There was a sound in Sumner's throat; Nightshade grinned grotesquely.

"I'm going to break you up good with this," he grated out, indicating the pickhandle he still held in his other hand. "You're going to go slow, bounty hunter."

Sumner realized what was happening now. A dark scowl crossed his aquiline face, and he carefully spat into Nightshade's right eye. Simultaneous with that act, he heard a sound outside the cabin and figured it was one or both of the others returning. Nightsade, enraged and livid as he wiped at his face, did not hear. He stepped back, and tightened his hold on the club with both hands. "Why, you piece of cow dung!" he gritted out.

Outside at that very moment, though, O'Brien had just ridden up, dismounted from his Appaloosa, and gone to the window to look inside, just as Sumner had earlier.

O'Brien was hunting shaggies east of town and had had a long day. He could not find a good place for hardship camp out there in the hills. He had known about the old Thurmond shack for a couple of years and had holed up in it one night last summer with McGraw. He had remembered it in late afternoon and had ridden there with the hope of finding one night's shelter. He had been surprised to find lights in the place and had come on in carefully to look things over.

Now, hunkering there beside the window in the darkness, O'Brien saw Nightshade standing in front of the tied-up Sumner and recognized Nightshade immediately as the buffalo hunter from years before that he thought he had killed in that Texas saloon.

"I'll be damned," he said under his breath.

Nightshade took one step back from Sumner and hefted the pick handle tightly; it was obvious to O'Brien what he intended to do.

O'Brien stepped quickly around to the door, which was closed. He touched it quietly and found it was barred from inside. He took a good hold on his Winchester rifle, and stepped back two paces, and charged into the wood door.

Inside, both men heard an explosive splintering of wood, and then the whole door came crashing loudly inward, torn from one of its leather hinges. It hit the wall hard to the left of the buffalo hunter. He stepped past it and stood there like some primordial savage, looking massive and dangerous in his bearskin coat and rawhides.

Nightshade whirled, his eyes widening in shock as he recognized O'Brien. "Holy mother!" he grated out.

His right hand released its hold on the club and quickly went for the Enfield Mark II revolver on his right hip. It had just cleared leather when O'Brien casually raised the Winchester and fired just once.

The room resounded with the yellow explosion, and hot lead snaked through Nightshade's right chest, missing his heart by an inch. He was thrown awkwardly backwards, flailing an arm against Sumner as he went running past him, his Enfield firing harmlessly into the ceiling as he went. He crashed over a chair and then hit the floor, staring up vacantly with his shark's eye, badly wounded.

O'Brien came on into the room, and Sumner watched him approach. He had never seen so big a man who was yet so athletic looking. He was two or three inches taller than Sumner and broad-shouldered. His square face under the handlebar mustache had a rugged, outdoor look to it, lines around his blue eyes put there by years of squinting into the glare of sun and snow, his flesh tanned by the heat of the plains and coarsened by trail dust.

"Looks like he had you in a hard place," O'Brien said.

Sumner felt something inside him release its clammy hand on his gut. He tried a grin and did not make it. "I had myself buried with quarters on my eyes," he grated out in pain. "Glad you came along, stranger."

"The name is O'Brien," the big man said.

Sumner squinted up at him. So this was the buffalo hunter whose name was as well-known in these parts as that of most gunfighters. "It's a pleasure . . . to know you, O'Brien."

O'Brien took a big bowie knife out from a stovepipe boot and cut Sumner loose. He was surprised when Sumner slumped to the floor. Sumner almost lost consciousness again. He felt big strong arms raise him up, drag him to a chair, then set him down on it. He kept his balance there.

"They beat on me," he said weakly. "I'm busted up."

O'Brien nodded. He walked over and looked down at Nightshade, who was bleeding badly from the chest wound. Nightshade looked up at O'Brien with his one eye and gave him a hateful look.

"No, I ain't dead, hunter," he said in a low voice. The one eye looked wild. "If you and me meet up again, you better watch your back. I'm going to feed you to the hogs the next time around."

O'Brien stared down at him. He raised the Winchester rifle slightly, aimed it at Nightshade's good eye, and squeezed the trigger.

The gun roared a second time in the close confines of the cabin, and a slug from its barrel ploughed into Nightshade's widened eye and on into his brain pan, blowing gray matter and bone all over the floor. Nightshade's arms and legs drummed at the floor rhythmically for a moment, and his trousers became wet at the crotch, and it was over.

"By God, that man was ugly," O'Brien said to himself.

Sumner had seen the execution, and his eyes narrowed down some on O'Brien, then he tried the smile again, and this time it worked. O'Brien had turned back to him. He made no mention of the new mess he had made on the floor across the room.

"How are you feeling?" he said.

"A lot better now," Sumner admitted, looking toward the corpse of Nightshade.

"We'd better get you to a medic," O'Brien said. "There used to be a sawbones right in town here." He jerked a thumb toward the dead outlaw. "Does he have friends?"

Sumner nodded. "And they're in Willard."

O'Brien shrugged the big shoulders under his coat. "What the hell. You can only die once."

Sumner grinned. "I couldn't have put it better myself."

Chapter Four

Very few people who had met Sumner ever got the chance to know what kind of man he really was. In the West in those days, men tended to classify other men in terms they could summarize in fifteen words or less. A lot of men came to the open territories because they were running from the law farther east or were trying to escape some other unpleasantness in past lives, and it was not considered good manners or even healthy to inquire too closely into a man's background. In many areas, you did not even ask a man's name. And, of course, Sumner was one of those who appreciated the privacy that those unwritten rules gave him.

Actually, Sumner was a man who had created himself out of a survival instinct. As a boy, he had not even liked guns. But when he had avenged the rape and murder of his aunt by killing the outlaw who had perpetrated those ugly crimes and then had been sent off to prison by a judge who wanted to teach him a lesson about the penalties of vigilanteism, Sumner had come out of confinement later to learn that the world looked upon him as a killer and a gunfighter. He had been required, therefore, to become what they already thought he was, just as a measure of self-defense. Then, just a short time after the Civil War, when he was still a kid, Sumner had met Clay Allison, and Allison had taken Sumner under his wing, so to speak, for a while. Allison had been a Southern-gentleman type, who had fought in the War Between the States as a Confederate, and it was he who taught Sumner to dress properly, drink in moderation, and shoot straight instead of just fast. Sumner slowly learned just what kind of fellow Allison was, through stories Allison himself told: Allison enjoyed killing a gunslinger who challenged him, and Sumner was put off by anybody who took pleasure in ending another man's life. Allison once pulled every tooth of a dentist who pulled the wrong tooth in Allison's mouth. He also once rode through a trail town stark naked and shot anybody who laughed at him. Sumner didn't like stories like that. So he drifted away from the other gunfighter. Later, just a few years ago, he heard that Allison had been run over by a freight wagon, crushed to death in a freak accident with his gun in its holster.

Sumner had tried working for an express agency and then had gone to gambling as a profession, but his past kept catching up with him. So he decided to use his gun to make a living and stay within the law. That meant hunting men for the bounties on their heads, and, since he always went after the big prizes, he was almost always after the very worst outlaws, men to whom he did not give an even break when he caught them, men he did not take alive. The best break they got was the opportunity to reach for leather and draw down on him.

What other men did not know about Sumner, because they never got past the guns, was that he was a rather sensitive, rather intellectual young man who read every book on which he could get his hands in the privacy of his hotel rooms, who liked musical presentations when he could attend them and always had a newspaper tucked into his saddlebag somewhere. He knew that there was a persecution of Jews in Russia that year, that Mexican farmers were complaining to President Porfirio Diaz about their lands being stolen by large landowners, and that the Dowager Empress Tsu Tzi was consolidating her imperial power in China and threatening to abrogate the Tientsin Treaty that allowed European missionaries in her country. But Sumner rarely ran into anybody with whom he could discuss matters like that, so he just kept his own counsel and let the world see him as it wanted.

O'Brien was very different. He had had no opportunity for self-education, and, although very smart in a practical way, he had no inclination to learn what was going on in the big outside world east of the Mississippi. Every bit of knowledge O'Brien had acquired was directed at hunting, killing, and survival. He knew things the Indians knew about the land, and survival on it, and he knew some of it better than they did. What he knew about other men was largely negative. Most of the trouble he had gotten into in his thirty-odd years had been in some town or other where he had gone to buy provisions or sell hides and skins. At two inches over six feet, wearing rawhides and appearing very uncivilized, O'Brien was the kind of man for whom ordinary townfolk stepped aside on the street and in stores. But his size and looks were a challenge to certain kinds of men: gunslingers, drifters, and wild cowboys. So O'Brien had had to defend himself regularly from various kinds of verbal and physical assault, and he had hardened inside some. He would never kill casually or without good cause. But if a man crossed O'Brien or threatened him in any substantial way, he had bought himself a peck of trouble. If a person threatened O'Brien's life and O'Brien took it seriously, O'Brien counted that threat just the same as if the adversary had drawn a gun to kill him. That was why Nightshade had not survived their encounter at the shack.

Other hunters, though, had learned that O'Brien would risk his own life to help another man in trouble and that if O'Brien told you he would do something, his word was as good as a gold double eagle. To the very few who had been allowed to get close to him, therefore, his friendship was valued beyond measure.

Sumner, surprisingly, had come close to achieving that status. O'Brien had saved his life, and O'Brien always felt a particular closeness to such a person, even without any further sociability. That was why he came to visit Sumner at his hotel room in Willard, the day after Sumner had been treated by a local doctor for his injuries.

As for Billy Lobo and Cuesta, they were long gone. They had been instructed by Gabriel not to get into any trouble until they all met up again in Stinking Creek. So when they got back to the cabin late the night before and found Sumner gone with the place torn up and Nightshade dead, they decided to find another hideout until things blew over and rode off to a nearby town.

Sumner was sitting up in bed, reading a newspaper that had been brought to him by the management, when he heard the knock on the door and saw O'Brien enter.

"Well. I wondered if I'd see you again." Sumner was bare chested, with a sheet drawn up to his waist. A lock of dark hair fell onto his forehead. He had a big bandage across his side and chest, one around his head, and a small one across his left cheek. His left arm was bruised, but not broken. The biceps had turned a blue-green color.

O'Brien looked him over, then closed the door behind him. He came over to the bed. He did not look quite as wild or formidable this morning as he had when he busted into that cabin. He had shed the furry coat and stood in his rawhides only. His stovepipe boots were cleaned of mud and dust, and, when he removed the Stetson, his thick hair was slicked back neatly and the brief handlebar mustache had been combed out. Sumner was impressed by the intelligent-looking blue eyes in the square face and by O'Brien's quiet, unassuming manner.

O'Brien drew up a straight chair. "You don't look as bad as I thought you might." He had carried his Winchester into the room, and he now stood it against the nearby wall. Sumner glanced at it and saw how the metal gleamed on it. It was well-kept.

"I've been worse off," Sumner said. His own gun hung on one of the bedposts, near his head. "But if you hadn't come along when you did, it would have been my corpse smelling up that cabin this morning."

"There's no trace of any gunmen in town," O'Brien told him. "They must have went."

"It's just as well," Sumner said, moving and making a face. "I'm in no shape to take them on just now."

O'Brien grinned slightly. "So you're Certainty Sumner. The management told me about you."

Sumner nodded. "And you're O'Brien. I guess the things they say about you aren't exaggerated."

O'Brien's blue eyes went somber. "I'm sure most of it's snake shit," he commented.

Sumner laughed softly, and then his aquiline face became serious, too. "I owe you one, O'Brien. Any time you need a favor, remember me. I'd appreciate the chance to repay your saving my skin."

"Hell," O'Brien said, "you don't owe me nothing, Sumner. Nobody ever owes nobody nothing. It ain't that kind of world."

Sumner studied O'Brien's rugged face. "There's

a bounty on that piece of shit out at the cabin. It's yours if you want it."

O'Brien shook his shaggy head. "I never took no money for killing a man. Suppose I never will."

Sumner regarded him with interest. "You must not think a lot of my chosen profession."

O'Brien shrugged. "If I thought about it, I guess I wouldn't."

There was a silence between them, then: "Sometimes a man is forced into a mold other people make," Sumner told him.

O'Brien did not like gunfighters of any variety. They all seemed to be out to prove something, even some of the lawmen, like the Earps. "I hear that's what Jesse James tells his maw," he said, holding Sumner's gaze.

Sumner laughed again. People did not talk to Sumner like that. Not after they knew who he was. He was beginning to like O'Brien.

"I guess that is an easy answer," he said.

"Are you aiming to gun down the Gabriels?" O'Brien said.

Sumner nodded. "Luther Gabriel is one of the few really bad men left in this territory right now, along with the people he hangs out with. You've got to ride clear over to Tombstone to run into any of the Clantons, and Wyatt Earp has that situation in hand, anyway. If Sheriff Behan will keep out of his way. Wes Hardin is in Huntsville Prison, and John Ringo and Bill Longley are there to keep him company. Even Big Nosed Kate has been run out of business by Doc Holliday. In another ten years, I'll have to go to clerking for a living."

77

"I tried working on a loading dock once, as a kid," O'Brien said. "I was clumsy as a hog on ice. I think you'd do about as well clerking in a store."

"You size a man up pretty well," Sumner said. "I guess we're both cut out for hunting. Of one kind or another."

"I guess so." O'Brien rose from the chair and retrieved the Winchester from the wall, tucking it under his arm. Suddenly he looked dangerous again. Sumner stared for a moment, wondering if even he would be able to count on survival in a confrontation with the buffalo hunter. If the story the bartender told was true, O'Brien had walked right through a hail of lead to beat a man to death. Looking at him now, Sumner believed the story.

"Well, I just thought I'd pay my regards. The weather is warming up. There's shaggies out there somewhere and I've got to find them."

Sumner rose painfully from bed, throwing the sheet off. He wore only a long underwear pants and was barefooted. He held his hand out to O'Brien. "I hope our trails cross again."

O'Brien took his hand in a big one, and Sumner felt like he had stuck it into an iron vise. "It ain't likely," O'Brien said.

Then, a moment later, he was gone.

Later that day, in early evening, Luther Gabriel and his demented brother Coot sat together in the one saloon in Stinking Creek. It was Saturday night, and there was a lot of traffic in and out of the place. There were cowboys and drifters and quite a

78

few locals. Gabriel had just come down from an upstairs bedroom where he had paid for and received a wild sexual encounter with one of his favorite whores, a heavy-set girl named Buxom Betty. It was said that Betty knew seventeen different ways to give a man sexual pleasure. Betty had a sliding scale of charges for her work, depending on the exotic nature of the sex act and the time it involved, and very few patrons had ever tasted the exquisite sweetness of the highest priced delicacy on Betty's repertoire of sensual extravaganzas. Most men did not even know exactly what the most exotic acts involved, for Betty swore her high-paying customers to secrecy.

With Luther Gabriel, though, it was different. Betty knew Gabriel's reputation, and he had verified it on one occasion by beating her badly before leaving her. He knew all of her delights well, and he paid when he felt like it. Betty never complained about him to management or to the local sheriff, Emmet Webster.

The Gabriels took a table in a corner of the place to try to avoid some of the loud talkers, and they were nursing a bottle of Planter's Rye. A cowboy with a wide, white Stetson came over and waved his own bottle at them.

"Have a drink from mine, boys! It's smooth as glass and warm as a woman's crotch!"

Gabriel looked up darkly. "Go shove that bottle up your ass, cowpoke," he growled.

The cowboy, despite his inebriation, saw something in Gabriel's eyes that sobered him slightly. "Hell. I didn't mean no trouble." He turned and went to another table.

Gabriel turned to Coot. "I wormed some information out of that whore that kind of interested me."

"Yeah?" Coot responded. His rather thin, pale face sagged with the beginnings of inebriation. His vacant-looking eyes regarded his older brother dully. He was wearing a heavy wool shirt and a dark vest over it, and all of his clothing looked soiled and wrinkled. Gabriel tried to get him to take a bath a couple times a year but was not always successful.

"There's this express agent lives on the edge of town north of here. Lives in back of the station with his kid. Name of Seger. The whore says she heard he's got money stashed away there. I had to knock her around to get it out of her, but it verifies what I heard before."

Coot's face brightened some. "How much money?"

"Nobody knows. But it could be a lot. He makes good wages."

"Well, let's go get it!" Coot exclaimed. But then his face clouded over and recaptured the vacant look. "Wait a minute. You said we'd wait here for the others. We go out there, it could cause us trouble here."

It always surprised Gabriel when Coot showed the slightest reasoning power. "I know. But things are getting unsettled hereabouts, anyway." He had just gotten a wire from Billy Lobo that Nightshade had been killed and they had had to flee to Bingham. "I'll get in touch with Billy and tell him and Cuesta to stay put in Bingham, and we'll meet them there."

"So we'll go out there?" Coot Gabriel said in his high, reedy voice, looking excited again.

"I think we just will," Gabriel said. He sat bulky and square on his chair, the pink scar on his cheek glowing in the light from the brightly lighted room. They both wore their trail-colored hats. Gabriel wore a sheepskin jacket over a heavy shirt. On his boots were big, Mexican spurs. He looked like the kind of man you kept away from, if you had any sense at all.

"Can we go tonight?" Coot went on. "Can we, Luther? Let's go out to Seger's place right now!"

Behind Gabriel, at another table, an older man heard Coot and narrowed his bushy-browed eyes on him.

"Keep your voice down, for Christ's sake!" Gabriel growled harshly at his brother. He lowered his some more. "Hell, yes, we'll go tonight. Just try to keep from yelling it out to the world, will you?"

A few moments later they had left, mounted up, and headed out for the railway express station run by O'Brien's friend, Aaron Seger.

At that same time, Seger was sitting in his living room at the rear of the station building, reading a Kansas City newspaper. He had had a long day with two freight trains coming through, and now he was relaxing before going off to bed. He was just reading an article about the abolishment of flogging in the British Navy, when Annie came out of her bedroom in her long nightgown. She came over and kissed him on the cheek, and Aaron smiled up at her.

"I'm going to bed, Daddy. Don't stay up too late."

"I won't, Annie," he told her.

"I'm going to write O'Brien a letter before I go to sleep," she said. "To thank him for the buffalo robe."

Seger smiled. "That's a nice idea. He keeps a post office box at Albuquerque. Trouble is, he sometimes don't get there for six months or a year."

"I don't care," she said. "It will be fun just writing it and thinking he'll get it later."

"You go ahead, then. Tell him I said to keep his soda biscuits dry."

"I will, Daddy."

Annie disappeared into her bedroom then, and Seger sat and puffed at a corncob pipe, reading another article from the Kansas City paper. He was halfway through it, relaxed and comfortable, when he heard the riders outside his door. He looked up and frowned. He was not expecting anyone that late at night. He put the paper down, knocked his pipe out, and rose from his chair. A knock came at the door.

"Hey, Seger! You in there?"

It was the deep, gruff voice of Luther Gabriel, but Seger had never heard it before. He went to the door, suspenders hanging down from his waist, with only long underwear above the belt. He opened the door cautiously and peered out.

He saw the big, scarred face of Gabriel looming

82

there, then the door was jammed farther open, and Gabriel and Coot came in, shoving Seger aside.

"Hey, what the hell!" Seger blustered, looking suddenly scared.

Coot closed the door after them and latched it as Gabriel turned to confront Seger, his dark eyes hard.

"Nice little setup you got here, Seger," Gabriel growled.

"Who are you? What do you want here?" Seger said breathlessly.

Gabriel grinned a brittle grin. "You see this fellow beside me here?" he said slowly, jerking a thumb at Coot. "You ask too many dumb questions, he'll take a bite out of you somewhere."

Seger's face sagged into heavy lines. "You're the Gabriels, aren't you?"

Coot grinned broadly, but Gabriel didn't. "I knowed this brother of mine since he sucked. And he gets awful ornery if somebody gets crossways of him like you're doing." Gabriel went on. "That right, Coot?"

Coot's grin disappeared, and he nodded. "Ask him where the money is," he said.

"Money?" Seger said. "I ain't got no money here, except for a few dollars for personal expenses. You come to the wrong place for money." He glanced involuntarily toward Annie's door, fear building in him. He was telling the truth about the money. He had about eleven dollars in the place.

Gabriel drew a Schofield .45 revolver from its holster and stuck it up against Seger's chest. "Now

83

listen to me, mister. We ain't going to play no games with you. You understand?"

Seger swallowed back his rising fear. "You can't come in here and hooraw me in my own place like this! I'm telling you the truth. Now please just leave and—"

At that moment, Annie appeared at the opened doorway to her room, frowning toward them.

"Who is it, Daddy?" she said with concern, looking from Gabriel to Coot.

They all looked toward her. Coot let a slow grin settle onto his narrow features. "Well, well," he croaked out. "Look what we got here. This must be the kid."

Gabriel glanced at Coot. "Keep her out of this," he said.

Annie saw the gun pointed at Seger and started toward him. Coot met her halfway and grabbed her by the arm.

"Let go of me!" she yelled at him, struggling.

"Leave her alone, damn you!" Seger said loudly. He started toward Coot, and Gabriel slugged him up alongside the head. He fell to the floor, grunting.

Annie screamed, and Coot dragged her back to the doorway and through it. The door slammed after them, and Seger could hear Annie still screaming in the other room.

Gabriel pulled Seger to his feet and slammed him down hard onto the straight chair near them. Blood wormed down the side of Seger's face, and he was only half-conscious now. "Annie—"

"Listen to me, you sonofabitch," Gabriel hissed

84

at him, the Schofield aimed at his face now. "You level with us about the money you got stashed here, or you're a dead man."

"There—ain't no money here," Seger choked out. "All I got's in that box over there on the sideboard. Just take it and leave us alone."

Gabriel went to the sideboard and opened up the wooden box he found there, a cigar box that said "Tampa Supremes" on its lid. He took some silver coins out and counted them.

"There's only a little over ten dollars here," Gabriel said. He came back over to Seger. "You're getting me riled, express man."

"I told you," Seger grunted out. "Please. Take it and let us be."

Gabriel was very angry. He hit Seger with the gun again, knocking him off the chair. A blackness welled in on Seger as he lay groaning on the floor.

"Now talk, damn you," Gabriel barked at him.

In the bedroom now at that same moment, Coot was just forcing Annie to the bed, and she was kicking at him with bared legs. She looked awfully good to Coot; he liked them young and virginal. Now Annie's youthful nudity was exposed to him right up to her waist, and he grew a quick lust for her. She was yelling again, so Coot cuffed her alongside the face and almost knocked her out. Then he unfastened his trousers in the sudden silence and mounted her, forcing a hard union that tore at Annie's flesh. She cried out again, but it was a muffled cry that time, and then Coot was raping her, taking her virginity.

Out in the bigger room, Gabriel had now kicked Seger in the side, the back, the chest. Seger was almost out, but in a lot of pain. "Where do you keep the goddam money?" Gabriel yelled down at him. He had already searched the station office up front and had rummaged around some more in the living room and without success.

Seger hardly heard him. His fevered brain only worried about his child now, because he could not hear her yelling any more.

"Annie," Seger mumbled.

"Oh, hell," Gabriel said in disgust. He aimed the Schofield casually at Seger's chest and pulled off a round. Seger jumped hard on the floor and died there.

Coot came back into the room, buckling his belt. He glanced down at Seger. "There weren't no money?"

Gabiel glared at him. "How would you know? Can't you keep that feeble mind on business for even a few minutes?"

Coot grinned. "Money ain't the only thing worth the taking."

"Well, there ain't any here, by Jesus. Let's ride."

Coot looked down at Seger and pulled a razor-sharp bowie knife from his belt. "Just give me another minute, brother. I'll catch up."

"Oh, Jesus," Gabriel growled. But he always humored his retarded sibling whenever he could. "Just hurry it up." He turned then and left, leaving Coot grinning over the corpse of the express agent.

Chapter Five

Certainty Sumner arrived in Stinking Creek a few days later, still sore from his beating at the hands of the Gabriel gang. His ribs were still taped under his shirt, and he had a new shallow scar across his left cheek.

Sumner's only motivation for going after the Gabriels, before his encounter with them, had been monetary. Now, though, it was different. Sumner was not the kind of man you beat on without killing. He had a score to settle now, and he would not rest easy until Luther Gabriel and his people were pushing up daisies at some boot hill somewhere.

He still had a deep soreness in his left arm and was glad it had not been his right one they had bruised. He could not afford for anything to hamper his gun hand in his business. A split-second difference in reaction time, under certain circumstances, could mean the difference between survival and sudden death.

Sumner hitched up outside the Prairie Hotel at about midday on his arrival, went in, and checked in at the desk. The place had a real carpet on the floor in the reception area, so Sumner knocked some slushy snow off his boots at the entrance. There was a dusty oil painting on the wall behind the desk above the bank of boxes for room keys that depicted a gunfight on horses between cowboys and what looked like Apaches. It looked like an early Remington, but Sumner could not see a signature on it.

Sumner checked in with a rather small, bespectacled fellow wearing a polka-dotted vest over a stiff-collar shirt and cravat. He looked Sumner over carefully while Sumner signed the register.

When Sumner was finished, he leaned on the counter of the desk for a moment. "I'm here looking for some men."

"Yeah?" the small man said, peering over the gold rims of the spectacles.

"Luther Gabriel and some men with him," Sumner said. He laid a double eagle on the wood counter. "I can pay for information."

The other man picked up the gold coin and turned it over in his hand, then bit it. He nodded to Sumner. "They been here," he said.

"Are they still around?" Sumner said.

The clerk shook his head. "They're long gone. That Gabriel and his brother. But not before they killed the express agent out at the edge of town."

Sumner's eyes narrowed down. "They've murdered again?"

"They shot him down in cold blood, according

to the town sheriff. They were drinking it up one night down at the saloon. They disappeared from there early, and then the next morning a neighbor found Seger. There were hoofprints there that the sheriff says match those of Gabriel's mount. And they kind of left a calling card." He smiled an irritating smile.

"What do you mean?" Sumner said.

"There were—pieces cut off of Seger," the clerk said, seeming to enjoy the telling. "The sheriff knows the details, you better ask him."

Sheriff Webster and Sumner had met before, and Sumner did not like him. He was very close-mouthed toward bounty hunters. "Is that all you know?" he said to the clerk. "When did they leave, and where did they ride out to? Anybody know?"

"Like I said, you better ask the sheriff," the clerk said smugly.

Sumner sighed. He threw his saddlebags and saddle blanket onto the counter. "Here. Take these up to my room. You can earn that twenty dollars that way, maybe."

He turned then and left the hotel, walking down to the sheriff's office, past the saloon where Gabriel and Coot had drank together that bloody night. He would stable the black stallion later. He walked up to the stucco building that had a sign on its front reading simply: Jail. He went inside. There was a barren desk and a straight chair, but nobody in sight. He glanced at a wanted poster on the nearby wall and read it.

Billy the Kid. $500 Reward. I will pay $500 reward to any person or persons who will capture

William Bonney, alias The Kid, and deliver him to any sheriff of New Mexico. Satisfactory proofs of identity will be required. Lew Wallace, Governor of New Mexico.

Sumner smiled and remembered his old friend Pat Garrett and his vow to be the one to kill Bonney. The poster was an old one, because the price had gone up on Bonney's head. Sumner walked to a doorway to some jail cells at the rear of the building and found Webster back there, cleaning up one of the cells. In a far cell in a dark corner sat a black man, looking half-asleep.

Webster peered up at Sumner and squinted down at him. He was middle-aged with a beard and sideburns. At the moment he looked more like a janitor than a lawman.

"Can I do something for you?" he said in a low voice. He was middle-aged, and there was some gray in the beard.

"Sheriff," Sumner said, "I came to ask about Luther Gabriel."

Webster came out of the cell, holding a folded blanket. "Oh. It's Sumner, is it?"

"I hear Gabriel caused you some trouble here recently."

Webster nodded. "Yep, he was here again. Hanging out at the saloon with that moron brother of his. Went out and killed a good friend of mine. Aaron Seger."

"I heard," Sumner said. "I guess you didn't have a chance to arrest him before he went out there."

Webster gave him a look and elbowed past Sumner to return to the front room of the place. He

90

put the blanket in a cabinet there, then went and sat on the edge of the desk.

"When that crowd is in town, I keep out of their way," he said blandly, holding Sumner's gaze steadily. "That's how I manage to stay alive to get the job done here." He had deep-set eyes the color of granite.

"I'm not here to say how you should have handled it," Sumner said in a flat tone. But he despised lawmen who took the pay and didn't do the job. If Webster was afraid of gunslingers, he should be clerking in a store somewhere. "I just wonder if you can tell me any more about the killing and maybe where you think Gabriel rode off to."

Webster gave him a sour look. "That ain't none of your business, bounty hunter. Not until you decide to put a badge on."

Sumner's face sobered. "If I'd been here that night wearing a badge, I wouldn't have to go riding out after Gabriel now," he said evenly.

Webster's face darkened with anger. "Now look here, mister—"

"Shut up, Sheriff," Sumner said.

"What!"

"You avoided trouble with Gabriel. Now do you want to make some with me? Do you feel awfully lucky today, Sheriff?"

Webster heard the tone in Sumner's voice, and he glanced down at Sumner's waist, toward where the Colt revolver hung across Sumner's flat belly. He sighed and went and sat on the chair behind the desk.

91

"Okay, don't get on your high horse." He looked down at his hands. "Gabriel must have thought Seger kept money out there. I could have told him he didn't. When he didn't get any, he shot Seger in the heart."

"That sounds like Gabriel."

"That ain't the half of it. The body was mutilated."

"Oh?"

"Seger was scalped. And there was a couple of parts cut off of him. Some meat off the left arm and one of his thighs. We figure that that was Coot."

Sumner shook his head.

"The girl was raped, too. Can you imagine, twelve years old?"

"Did they kill her?" Sumner asked.

"No, but they might as well have. She's over at the sanitorium at Albuquerque. Don't say nothing, don't see nothing, don't hear nothing. Just sets and stares. It's all kind of pitiful."

Sumner sighed heavily.

"Seger knew some buffalo hunter named O'Brien," Webster went on. Sumner focused on him again. "The girl Annie was writing him a letter that night and never finished it."

Summer could hardly believe how O'Brien's life kept touching his in past weeks. "O'Brien?" he said. "Are you sure?"

"I got the letter," Webster told him.

"Can I see it?"

Webster gave him a look, then fished in a desk drawer, rifling through some papers there. He came up with a wrinkled piece of paper and handed it to Sumner. Sumner read the careful longhand:

> Dear O'Brien,
>
> We hope you are well out there on the plains and that you have found a big herd by now. Aaron says the hunting is better for you in the good weather, so I prayed for a big thaw the other night.
>
> I put the robe right next to my bed, and it looks real nice there. I never had as nice a gift, and I wanted to thank you again for it. Aaron thanks you, too. I think of you each time I look at it.
>
> We have had some Spanish influenza here, and old man Ryker died of it. So far we are healthy here at the station, though. With spring coming, we are looking forward to the warm weather and wildflowers. I just know that 1881 is going to be our best year yet here, and I thank God that

Sumner looked up from the paper, staring past Webster.

"She didn't get to finish it," Webster said. "We figure that she was writing it when Gabriel arrived. It's a real tragedy."

Sumner looked at Webster and found little real empathy in his bearded face. "I've met this O'Brien and know what he looks like," he said. "Mind if I keep this to deliver to him, if I see him again?"

Webster hesitated, then shrugged. "Hell, keep

it. She'll never miss it, poor kid."

Sumner stuck the letter into a pocket, folded. "You have any idea where Gabriel might have ridden out to?"

"Sure. They headed out southeast. They'll probably meet up with the rest of the gang down there somewhere after this blows over."

Sumner gave him a sober look. "Will it blow over?"

"If you're asking me if I'm going after the likes of Gabriel, the answer is no," Webster said slowly. "I don't mind some risk on this job, but I don't have no hankering for suicide. He's killed a half-dozen sheriffs already, hereabouts."

"Three," Sumner corrected him.

"Three, six. I'm a town sheriff, Sumner. I'm small-time law. Let the federal marshals and the big county sheriffs with the big salaries go after him. I ain't no goddam gunfighter." He eyed Sumner's gun again hostilely.

"Is there going to be a reward offered from here to add to what's already on his head?" Sumner asked him.

Webster shook his head. "Is that all you bounty people ever think about, them big rewards?"

Sumner came over to him, around the desk, and stood ominously beside him. "I asked you a question, Webster," he said.

Webster looked terrified suddenly. "No, there's no move to raise the ante."

"You better be leveling with me, Sheriff."

"I'm telling you what I know."

Sumner turned and walked to the door, opening

94

it. Before he left, he spoke once more to the sheriff. "Why don't you take that badge off and let somebody wear it who will make some use of it?" he said in a hard voice.

The sheriff did not reply to that.

He figured Sumner did not really expect a response, anyway.

April had finally arrived in the territory, later, when O'Brien rode into Duran one sunny morning to buy some supplies.

The last few weeks had provided fairly good hunting. O'Brien had just sold off a stack of high-quality hides, and now he needed a replenishment of grub, ammunition, and odds and ends.

Duran was just a one-street town for the most part, but it boasted a sizeable general store, a rather primitive saloon, and even a small bank. There were a couple of ranches nearby, and cowboys frequented the places of business and kept them going.

O'Brien picketed his Appaloosa at the hitching rail outside the store and climbed off the mount. Because O'Brien was big, the horse was big, and its gray flanks now glistened slightly in the sun because O'Brien had ridden in from a distance, starting before sunup that morning.

O'Brien stood tall beside the horse as he looked into a saddlebag for a moment, and then climbed a couple of steps up to the store entrance. He wore the rawhide shirt and pants, and his brown hair was rather long under the trail-colored Stetson. He had three guns on his mount's irons, but was carrying none of them at the moment. A large hunting knife stuck out of his right boot, the one with which he skinned buffalo.

Behind the Appaloosa was tied a long-eared mule, a pack animal that carried the hides O'Brien had recently sold and would be used to haul a wagon when O'Brien had purchased another one. The mule watched O'Brien stop at the head of the steps and look at the saloon entrance down two doors. O'Brien turned and walked to the saloon, hesitated, and returned to his mount. He pulled the Winchester out of its saddle scabbard and tucked it under his right arm. It was one thing to go into a store unarmed and quite another to enter a drinking place. He had found that out down in Texas one night, when he had had to defend himself against a gun with his fists. That was the time he had killed his assailant by beating him to death.

Moments later O'Brien entered the saloon. He started for the bar to order a whiskey when he heard the booming voice call to him from the rear of the place.

"O'Brien! Over here, you sonofabitch!"

O'Brien knew it was McGraw even before he turned and spotted him, rising from a rear table and hobbling over to him. He was limping on the leg that had been gored by the buffalo the last time O'Brien had seen him. O'Brien met him halfway, and they just stood and grinned at each other for a long moment.

"You look almost human," O'Brien said to him

in his deep voice. "You must have got some good doctoring."

McGraw's beefy face beamed through the gray beard. He was bareheaded, and the wild gray hair around his face gave him a very primitive look. A customer came in, saw the two savage-looking men standing in the middle of the room, and shied off around them.

"I took your advice and saw a vet in Fort Garland." O'Brien had split with him before they got there. "He fixed me up nice. I just threw away the cane he gave me. Come on over to the table, I got news for you, pardner!"

O'Brien nodded and turned to a heavyset bartender. "Bring us a bottle of your best whiskey, barkeep."

The bartender gave him a sour look. He never liked to see a buffalo hunter come in. They stank and they scared other customers away. "Coming right up," he said balefully.

O'Brien went over to McGraw's table with him, and they sat down there. The bartender came and left them a second bottle—McGraw had already mostly finished a partial one—and left them alone. He went and attended to another couple of customers at the long bar.

McGraw leaned in toward O'Brien as O'Brien opened the whiskey and poured each of them a shot of it. O'Brien took a long, heavy swig from the bottle itself. He set the bottle down and wiped at his mouth with his rawhide sleeve. The Winchester was propped beside him against the table.

"I seen it, O'Brien," McGraw said in a low, hoarse whisper.

O'Brien studied McGraw's face and saw the emotion in it that had escaped him on the first assessment. McGraw was worked up but trying to keep himself under control.

"Huh?" O'Brien said.

"I seen the goddam albino."

O'Brien squinted down. "Oh. The white buffalo again."

"I went out to the Chaco by myself." His voice became reverential, as if he were speaking of a religious experience. "He was in a herd of about fifty animals. I wish you could of seen him, O'Brien. He's white as Irish linen and big as a mountain."

O'Brien stared past McGraw for a moment, imagining that.

"He was just hanging out with this small herd till he got something better to do," McGraw went on. "He'd killed the bull leader—I found the corpse about a half-mile away." He shook his head slowly. "He tore that animal up something awful, O'Brien. There wasn't nothing left of it but horns and hooves."

"What happened? Did you get a shot?"

McGraw nodded, and O'Brien thought he saw his hand tremble just slightly. "I got two good shots at him. Right at the heart." He looked up and held O'Brien's gaze. "Nothing happened."

"What?"

"I'm telling you. It was like he wasn't touched. Like the lead went right through him without touching him, O'Brien."

"Oh, bullshit, McGraw." O'Brien swigged the shot glass of whiskey.

McGraw looked angry. "I was there, goddam it!" he said, raising his voice some. "I should of hit that animal. Twice."

O'Brien shook his shaggy head and touched his mustache with a muscular hand. "You was crippled up, pardner. Teetering on one good leg. You're lucky you didn't shoot yourself in the foot."

McGraw spoke more slowly. "I got two good shots in. That sonofabitch ought to gone down." He stared at his own shot glass. "Some are saying that you'd have to hit him with a special bullet. Or maybe he can't be killed at all."

"I ain't seen no shaggy yet that didn't go down if you hit him right," O'Brien said. "That's all just blue smoke, McGraw. Puffed up by some drunken hunter that ought to be clerking for his pay."

McGraw looked down at his whiskey. "He come for me, O'Brien."

O'Brien shrugged. "He give you a better shot."

"He had blood in his eye," McGraw said. "They say he's killed four men, including an Apache. I got on my mount and kicked them spurs in. But he chased me, O'Brien. He *chased* me on my goddam horse. The animal's got the beast of Hades in him."

O'Brien poured himself another shot. "Sure."

McGraw leaned toward O'Brien again. "There's a story about him. I just heard it a few days ago, after the hunt."

"Yeah?" O'Brien said patiently.

"You ever heard of Luther Gabriel?"

O'Brien's interest quickened. He recalled Certainty Sumner. "I heard of him," he said.

"Well, this tale goes that Gabriel used to have an Indian with him, about a year ago. A Blackfoot, they say. Gabriel spotted the albino one day and took a shot at it. Same like with me, the lead just seemed to pass right through that beast. The Blackfoot was impressed and talked Gabriel out of firing again. Said some words in Blackfoot, like a priest might, then told Gabriel he couldn't be killed as long as that devil beast was alive, because there was some kind of spell between them now."

"McGraw—" O'Brien said heavily.

"And a lot of hunters is saying that Gabriel will go on rampaging through this territory, killing and mauling just like that damned devil beast, till some hunter with more magic from the dark place than that buffalo's got puts a chunk of hot silver right through his heart."

"Silver?" O'Brien said.

"I guess that notion come from the Blackfoot. There's a hunter down in Magdalena says the albino is out to get him." He paused. "Maybe it's the same with me. I don't know, O'Brien. I just wish you seen the look in them little red eyes when he come after me. I never saw the like."

"I don't think no shaggy's got the brains to remember who tried to put a bullet in him," O'Brien said. "And if they did, that would suit me right down to the ground." He looked McGraw over. McGraw looked older somehow. "Are you

100

really ready to hunt? I'm heading north for a while. There's a big herd reported up by Tres Piedras. If you still got that wagon, we could head up that way together. The weather is warming now, and the herds are coming back to the grasslands."

McGraw shook his head. "I sold the wagon. I needed the money to go after the albino. I'm heading back out there to find him."

"For God's sake," O'Brien grumbled.

"Listen, O'Brien, you don't know it all. Some Kansas City lawyer heard about the white shaggy. He put an ad in the paper; he'll pay a thousand dollars for the white robe."

O'Brien's blue eyes squinted down hard. "A thousand dollars?"

"I saw the paper myself," McGraw said. "You realize how much hunting a man would have to do, and skinning and curing, to make that much money?"

"I know," O'Brien assured him.

"Come with me, O'Brien," McGraw said in his low, gravelly voice. "I can find him again. There must be a way to kill him. Maybe we got magic to match the Indian's if we go together. One fellow says if we cast our own spell—"

"Goddam it, McGraw," O'Brien growled now. "You're crazy with this, you got the fever. You might not see that white buffalo for another year. Nobody plans a hunt around one goddam animal. I'm going north to Magdalena. If your white buffalo ever comes within our hunting range, I'll go after him with you."

McGraw rose slowly. "I'm sorry. O'Brien. I got to do this, it ain't something I got a choice over. I know you're a Webster on shaggies, there ain't no other man I'd rather ride with. But if you won't come with me, I'll go it alone till this thing's over."

O'Brien was nettled. "Suit yourself," he said.

McGraw thumped him on his broad shoulder and limped out of the place. O'Brien stared after him for a long moment, then turned toward the bartender. He was about to order some hard-boiled eggs, when two men came in through the slatted doors. One of them was Certainty Sumner.

Sumner saw O'Brien as soon as he entered and turned to the man with whom he had come in. That man was Pat Garrett. Sumner had just run into Garrett for the second time since the first of the year at Vaughan, nearby. Garrett was running down a lead on Billy the Kid, with whom he was obsessed now, and Sumner was trying to get a lead on the whereabouts of Luther Gabriel.

A couple of locals turned and glanced at Sumner and Garrett when they entered. Sumner had a new corduroy suit coat on over his red vest, and he sported a new blue cravat at the neck. Locals did not ordinarily see anyone quite so well dressed, not even the local banker. They also saw the Colt strapped across his belly.

Garrett wore dungarees and chaps, and a wool jacket over a thick shirt. He was currently sporting a long, ivory-handled revolver in an oiled holster on his right hip. They looked like a couple of men to whom one spoke carefully.

"There's somebody we both know," Sumner said to Garrett. "Come on over and let me reintroduce you." He remembered that Garrett had met O'Brien briefly a while back.

"You know that buffalo hunter?" Garrett said in surprise.

"Met him since we talked. He saved my life," Sumner said.

O'Brien watched them come. He had reckoned he would never see the gunfighter again. He pulled himself up out of a small depression about McGraw to give Sumner a grin. "Well. You look a mite better than when I seen you last."

"O'Brien," Sumner smiled his handsome smile. He noted the Winchester beside O'Brien's chair. "Pleased to see you again so soon. I told you our paths might meet again."

"You never know where the trail will lead you," O'Brien said. He glanced over at Garrett and did not recognize him.

"This here is Pat Garrett," Sumner said. "He's the law down in Lincoln County. He says you two met up once down that way."

O'Brien focused on Garrett. "Your face does look familiar, Sheriff. Was you in that Cattle War down that way?"

Garrett shook his head sidewise. "That got over about the time I arrived, O'Brien. But it created a killer named Bonney that still keeps me running after him."

"Mind if we join you?" Sumner said.

"Hell, no," O'Brien replied. But he preferred drinking alone. He generally did not enjoy the company of other men. "It's a free town, ain't it?"

Sumner and Garrett sat down at the table, and O'Brien noticed the scar still healing on Sumner's left cheek. It gave Sumner a rugged look that he had not had before. "The whiskey is on me, boys," O'Brien said. "If you don't mind Planter's."

"It suits me right down to my boots," Garrett grinned.

O'Brien called for two more glasses, and the bartender brought them. O'Brien poured out the golden liquid for Sumner and Garrett. Garrett swigged half of his and rolled some around on his tongue. He tipped his hat back on his head, hitched his thumbs into his belt, and the jacket was pulled back, showing his star. A cowboy nearby glanced at it balefully. A drifter at the bar, an enormous, ugly man, turned and regarded the threesome with a dour look.

Garrett was assessing O'Brien and his wild demeanor. "You still hunting buffalo, O'Brien?"

O'Brien nodded. "That's my trade, Garrett."

"I hear the herds are getting thinned out," Garrett continued. "How are the shaggies running this spring?"

"Thin," O'Brien said. He would wait a respectable time until they had drank some of his liquor, then he would excuse himself. He hated the talking and socializing other men found entertaining.

"Pat here thinks he might have a lead on the Kid," Sumner said, sipping at the whiskey.

"He's been a slippery little bastard," Garrett

said. "But Governor Wallace wants to see him hanged."

O'Brien looked over at him. "You don't hang a goddam rattlesnake," he said in the deep, level voice. "You mash it under your boot heel."

Both Sumner and Garrett liked that response. "My sentiments exactly," Garrett said.

"I have the same feeling about Luther Gabriel," Sumner admitted, "after my run-in with his boys. O'Brien saved my hide on that one."

Garrett regarded O'Brien seriously. "Sounds like you can take care of yourself, buffalo man. You ever think of pinning a badge on?"

O'Brien gave Garrett a hard, somber look and rose from his chair. He threw a few coins onto the table. "That pays for the bottle, boys. I'll be making tracks; I got a mount that needs livery." He picked up the Winchester and was about to turn to leave when the big, ugly drifter came over to their table.

"Where do you think you're going, buffalo man?"

O'Brien turned and eyed the fellow grimly. He knew he had stayed too long. There was always some jackass in a town who either wanted to talk you to death or call you out.

"You talking to me, mister?" O'Brien said.

"You see any other hunters in here that stink like buffalo shit?" the big fellow said. He was as tall as O'Brien and outweighted O'Brien by close to a hundred pounds. He was a mountain of a man, and he looked like he could eat a horse for dinner. He carried a long-barreled revolver on his left hip.

Sumner recalled his recent run-in with the drifters in Bernardo. It seemed like there were troublemakers everywhere, nowadays. He shook his head at the insult to O'Brien. "You realize that man across the table is wearing a badge?" he said to the drifter.

The ugly man made a sound in his throat. "Any lawman that would drink with the stink of buffalo around him can't be much of a goddam man," he growled. He had no idea he was talking to two of the fastest guns in the territory. He turned back to O'Brien. "Now, you apologize to every man in this room, buffalo man, for stinking up this nice saloon."

A silence had fallen over the room. A half-dozen other customers sat and stood around them, beginning to enjoy what was happening.

"Move your freight, snail slime," O'Brien growled in a voice so low and hard it was almost inaudible in the room.

The ugly man's face darkened with quick fury. "I'm going to bust your skull open like a goddam melon," he said, "then I'm going to shoot your goddam liver out." His hand went clumsily for his gun.

Garrett started to draw, but his move was unnecessary. While the drifter's hand was still clearing leather at his holster, O'Brien swung the Winchester across the ugly fellow's face. The barrel of the long gun cracked loudly there, breaking all the front teeth in the big fellow's mouth, mashing his nose flat, and smashing his jaw. The drifter's trigger finger pulled off an explosive round that shot into the floor at O'Brien's feet, and then the drifter hit the floor beside the table like a sack of salt, making the floorboards shake when he hit. O'Brien moved over to him as he scrabbled like a bug there and kicked him hard in the side, fracturing three ribs. A croaking sound came from the fallen man's throat. O'Brien kicked again, and there was a choking sound. The fellow's head rolled to one side. He had lost consciousness. There was a lot of spattered blood on the floor and teeth mixed in with it.

A customer at a nearby table whistled through his teeth. "Holy Christ!" he whispered.

O'Brien turned back to the table. "Good to see you again, Sumner." He then kicked a chair out of his way, breaking two of its legs as it crashed to the floor, and he strode out of the saloon with every eye on him.

Garrett holstered his sidearm and looked over at Sumner with narrowed eyes. "That's some buffalo man you met up with. Kind of antisocial, ain't he?" he grinned.

Sumner returned the grin. "I kind of understand though," he said. He, too, rose from the table. The bartender had come over to study the fallen drifter, who was still motionless.

"I've got some business with him, Pat. I'm going to follow him down to the livery stable. I'll meet you back here in an hour or so, and we'll have a meal together."

Garrett wondered why Sumner would want anything to do with an obvious savage like O'Brien. The two seemed like oil and water to him. "I'll be here," he said.

Down at the livery stable at the end of town, O'Brien had just delivered the Appaloosa stallion over to the hostler for a grooming and feeding. O'Brien had looked for Mustang McGraw when leaving the saloon, but McGraw had taken his hides and mount, it appeared, and ridden out already. That bothered O'Brien, because it seemed McGraw was setting himself on a downhill course, and O'Brien had come to like the old codger. O'Brien hoped McGraw got the white buffalo thing out of his system this spring and would be ready to do some real hunting again by summer. If so, and O'Brien ran onto him again, he would offer McGraw the chance to partner up with him again for awhile.

O'Brien had just given the hostler instructions about caring for the Appaloosa while O'Brien bought some supplies. He was leaving the stable building when Sumner caught him outside the big double doors.

"O'Brien. You got a minute?"

O'Brien regarded Sumner impatiently. "What is it, Sumner?"

Sumner came up to O'Brien and looked up slightly into his square face. "I understand you know a fellow named Aaron Seger."

O'Brien regarded him narrowly. "What if I do?"

Sumner sighed slightly. "I'm afraid I've got some bad news for you," he said. "I didn't want to mention it in there."

O'Brien's stomach tightened up slightly. "Bad news? What bad news?"

Sumner held his hard gaze. "Seger is dead, O'Brien."

"What?" O'Brien said hollowly. Seger had been the only tie O'Brien had with those early days in Tennessee. He had been the only man alive who had known O'Brien's father. "What the hell are you talking about?"

"It was Luther Gabriel," Sumner told him. "Him and that moron brother of his. They went to rob Seger—I heard it from the law at Stinking Creek. I just missed them there."

O'Brien stared hard at Sumner for a long moment, then he went and leaned against the side of the building. Sumner went over beside him and also leaned against the weathered planks.

"You're sure he's dead?" O'Brien said.

Sumner nodded. "The sheriff was sure. A guy named Webster."

"I know him," O'Brien said dully.

"There was some—mutilation," Sumner went on. "It seems Coot Gabriel is a goddam animal."

O'Brien's scowl deepened. "Sonofabitch," he growled.

"The girl—"

O'Brien turned quickly. "What happened to Annie?"

"She's alive. But she was raped."

O'Brien's face set itself into hard lines. "By

Jesus," he muttered in an almost inaudible voice.

Sumner went on carefully. "She—hasn't spoken a word since it happened. She's being kept at a place for—well, it's a kind of hospital in Albuquerque."

O'Brien squinted into Sumner's handsome face for a moment, then turned away, staring at the muddy ground. Sumner reached into a pocket and proffered a paper to O'Brien. It was Annie's letter to him. "I brought this for you. The kid was writing to you when—they came."

O'Brien took the paper and unfolded it. He stared at the writing for a moment, the looked over at Sumner helplessly. "I don't read so good."

O'Brien was asking for Sumner's help, and it was precisely that moment that Sumner began liking him. "Let me read it to you," he said quietly.

O'Brien nodded and handed the letter back to him. Sumner read it aloud. O'Brien listened silently until it was finished. Then he stared out over the tops of the bare aspen trees at the edge of town.

"It looks like I'm going to have to take some time out from tracking shaggies," he finally said.

Sumner had hoped for that response. He turned to O'Brien. "Look. I know what you said in Willard, about not being interested in bounties. But if you're going after Gabriel, you might as well accept the fact that the law would be mighty grateful if you killed him. I like your style, O'Brien. Can you shoot that Winchester as well as you can swing it against a man's head?"

O'Brien looked over as if he had just heard Sumner talking at the very end of all that. "Shoot?" he said in his deep voice. "Yeah, I can shoot." He was thinking of Gabriel, and when he spoke, it was rather to himself. "I can hit a shaggy's eye at five hundred yards downhill in a hailstorm." He was not boasting to Sumner, just telling himself what he would do to Gabriel if given the opportunity.

Sumner smiled to himself. "That's what I figured," he said. "The way I look at it, if you and I teamed up, we could bring Gabriel down together. He'll have other men with him. I could use some help when I go against his guns."

O'Brien looked over at him.

Sumner held the big man's gaze. Sumner had never seen a man so physically capable in appearance. O'Brien looked as if he could climb a mountain or wrestle a bear or run fifty miles through deep snow. Under the rawhides and wild demeanor, he was a magnificent physical specimen. Sumner himself was in good shape, but whereas Sumner was lithe, O'Brien was powerful; where Sumner was sinewy-tough, O'Brien was all gristle and bone and muscle. Sumner was a leopard, elusive, fast as lightning, deadly. O'Brien was a dark-maned lion.

"I don't think so," O'Brien finally told him.

Sumner frowned. "I'm offering you half of the bounties," he said. "If you're going to risk your neck anyway, let's do it right. Raise the odds a little. We're both after the same people."

O'Brien stepped away from the building wall,

inspected his rifle a moment, then looked Sumner square in the eye. "It's nothing against you, Sumner. It's me. I work best alone." He took the letter back and stuffed it into his belt. "I only hunted shaggies with one other man all this time. That's just the way it is."

O'Brien turned and walked away.

"There's a better chance of getting them all my way," Sumner said after him. "And you could use the bounties to help the girl."

O'Brien turned back to him with a scowl, and Sumner knew he had gone too far. O'Brien let his hard stare burn into Sumner's dark eyes for a long moment, then he left without another word.

Chapter Six

Luther Gabriel and his brother Coot arrived in Magdalena a short time later, the last week in April. The recent light snow had melted off the ground, and buds were popping out on the local elders and cottonwoods. The Gabriels were on their way to Bingham to meet up with Cuesta and Billy Lobo there, but they were in no hurry to get there. Gabriel wanted to have a plan for summer operations in mind when the four joined forces again, and he was having trouble deciding on one. The trouble was, Coot was no help at all and never had been. In fact, Coot would not have lasted five minutes with Gabriel if he had not been his younger brother. But as cold-blooded as Gabriel was, he had a feeling for this rather deranged sibling whom he had helped raise.

Magdalena was just another cowtown in central New Mexico with the usual dirt street and a double row of weathered clapboard buildings. There were a few hundred families living there permanently, and they had a saloon, two stores, and a gambling hall. Gabriel and Coot had ridden in about midmorning and hitched their mounts outside the latter establishment, because light meals were served there. The building had a high, false front with a big lettered sign that said simply, "Magdalena Gaming." It was set up three steps from street level and had an overhang over a porch with a log bannister railing. The swinging doors at the entrance and the elk's antlers over the doors gave the place a raffish, rakish look, making the interior seem pregnant with undisclosed pleasant secrets. An old sign hung on the facade, advertising nostrums, emetics, and balsams, from a time when the proprietor dispensed patent medicines. An entire cartload of the cure-alls had been left with the establishment by a traveling drummer who had ignored a smallpox quarantine in Las Cruces and had been brought down by a disease for which he had no remedy. On the other side of the entrance hung a smaller sign that announced: "ICE—A Penny A Pound."

Gabriel and Coot climbed the steps and entered the place. Gabriel stood and let the darker light open his pupils wide until he could see again. There were two billiards tables at the rear of the place and a faro table over on a side wall. Between the billiards tables and the entrance, where Gabriel and Coot stood, were four tables with straight chairs. Set into the wood tops of two of the tables were chess or checker boards in different colored woods. There was a caged-off area like a small office on the right with paneling up to waist level and crossed wire from there to the ceiling. An opening in the wire formed a wide window through which business was done. An attendant-clerk sat on a stool behind the window, wearing a green shade visor on his forehead. Attached to the wire cage was yet another sign, which read: "BEER 5¢, Sandwiches 50¢, Boiled Eggs 25¢."

Gabriel walked over to the cage and eyed a cash box on a ledge near the clerk. He figured there wasn't enough in it to bother with, and he would pass it up.

"Yes, sir. Care to play some pool?"

Gabriel eyed him soberly. If a man tried to ingratiate himself to Gabriel with courtesy or friendliness that just made Gabriel despise him. "No pool. What you put on them sandwiches?"

The clerk smiled nicely. He was a thin fellow with a triangular face and thin lips. His eyes had a watery look to them. He wore a stiff-collar shirt under a tan vest and had sleeve garters to keep his cuffs out of his way when he kept the records of sales for the day in a ledger on the counter behind the wire.

"Oh, we make nice sandwiches," the clerk said in his Kansas City speech. "We can give you beef or chicken, gentlemen. And set you up with a couple of cool glasses of beer with it."

"Make it two beefs and two beers," Gabriel said gruffly. "And don't take all day with it."

The clerk saw the harsh look of Gabriel's face, with its full beard and the scar on the left cheek, and glanced unobtrusively at the Wells Fargo revolver on Coot Gabriel's hip as Coot moved up

115

nearer his brother. "Anything you say, mister," the clerk said, the smile gone.

Gabriel and Coot adjourned to the nearest table. Gabriel kicked out the trail cramps from his legs as he sat down and turned toward the rear pool table, where two rough-looking young men were just starting a game.

"How can anybody waste their time knocking little balls around on a goddam tabletop?" Gabriel said in his gravelly voice.

Coot looked toward them. "Want me to get rid of them, Luther?"

"Just sit still and wait for your sandwich and beer," Gabriel growled at him.

The other men had begun their game, and in a few minutes, the attendant brought the Gabriels the beer and sandwiches. "Anything else, gentlemen?"

"Get away!" Coot hissed at him.

The fellow blanched slightly and went over to the billiards table. He glanced over his shoulder toward the Gabriels, then turned to the two other men. "Would either of you fellows like a nice cool beer?"

The two looked up from their game of eightball. They were both rather slim with one a bit taller and older looking. The younger one came around the table with a cue stick, grinning. "How much is that there beer?"

"Just a nickel a glass, boys. Ice cold."

The grin slid off the face of the young one. He and the other man were cowpokes, but out of work and just drifting around now, looking for a way to

116

survive. In a small town south of there, they had just held up an assayer's office and robbed it of five hundred dollars cash and three ounces of gold dust. The younger man had since decided he liked that better than cowboying.

"A nickel a glass?" the taller man said now, moving over toward the attendant. He gave his friend a sly wink. "You think we'd pay a nickel a glass for the slop you got in that back room?"

Gabriel and Coot paused in their eating to look over toward the threesome now. Gabriel shook his head slowly.

"Why, I just charge what the owner says, boys," the attendant was saying.

The young drifter grabbed the visor off the attendant's head, scaring the man. "What the hell you use this thing for? Staring down the front of the girls' dresses?" He laughed loudly and was joined by the other drifter.

"I'll just go quiet them down some, Luther," Coot said in his reedy voice.

"Goddam it, eat your sandwich!" Gabriel growled.

The attendant was surrounded by the drifters now and could not find an easy way to back off. "Boys, just let me get back to my office," he said. "If you don't want nothing, I've got some work to do over there."

"Work, hell," the young drifter said. "Let's see how you play pool."

The attendant shook his head. "I don't play the games with the customers, boys." He glanced around and realized that these two and the

Gabriels were the only people in the place, except him.

The young drifter grabbed the attendant by the shirt front now. "You telling me we ain't good enough to play pool with?" He reached for the long revolver on his hip with his other hand and stuck it up under the attendant's chin.

Gabriel sighed, swigged some beer, and rose from his table. He strode over to the pool table and moved up to the three men. He came up very close to the attendant. "Get to hell out of here and leave us alone," he said in his deep, gravelly voice.

The drifter who was holding him glanced at Gabriel, saw the looks of him, and released his hold on the attendant. The fellow looked from him to Gabriel, and hurried toward a back room, glad to be out of it. The older drifter gave Gabriel a hard look.

"That wasn't none of your business, mister."

Gabriel regarded him with dark, piercing eyes and made the other man wince inside under the look. "He was disturbing my eating," Gabriel said slowly. His look softened. "There's enough beer in that cooler back there for all of us, and there's no call to pay a penny for it. Why don't you join us for a drink?"

The younger fellow grunted softly. He holstered the gun. "Why should we? We got a game going here."

Gabriel looked over at him. "I got something more interesting to talk about than a goddam pool table can give you," he said.

The two drifters looked at each other, and the

older one shrugged. "Hell. Why not?" he said.

They came over to the Gabriels' table and introduced themselves all around. The older drifter was named Ross, and the younger one was called Cassidy. Coot went and got a pitcher from an ice chest and brought the beer to the table, along with two more tall glasses. Gabriel poured the newcomers some beer, and they all swigged the froth off the tops of the liquid. Gabriel wiped a sleeve across his beard.

"You two look like you're kind of drifting around the territory without much purpose in life," Gabriel said at last. "Am I right or wrong?"

"We got things to do," Cassidy said defensively.

Ross grunted. "You're right," he said. "So what?"

Cassidy was stealing glances at Coot. He had never seen such an ungainly fellow, with his long, greasy hair, and thin, bony face, and the eyes with the vacant stare.

"So I figured you boys as somebody that would like to make some quick cash and not worry much about what you had to do to get it," Gabriel said.

The older fellow squinted some at Gabriel. "Hey. I know your name now. You're wanted by the law all over this territory."

"Does that bother you?" Gabriel said. Since he had lost Nightshade to that buffalo hunter—he had heard from a stage driver how O'Brien had saved Sumner from Nightshade in Willard—he had realized that he had to expand the gang again, if he really intended to do some big things in the spring and summer.

119

"No," the older drifter said. "It don't bother us none."

Cassidy glanced at him, fog wisps of mild uncertainty clouding red-rimmed, hostile eyes. His clothing fit badly on his skinny frame. An odor of stale sweat emanated from his shirt collar where it was open.

"Good," Gabriel told them. "Me and brother Coot here is the ones that took that bullion train at Bernardo. Us and a couple others we ride with."

Ross nodded. "They been laying it on you. I guess they had it reckoned right." His narrow-brimmed homburg-type hat sat incongruously on a long, lean face that boasted a rather large, hooked nose. He and Cassidy were a rather odd-looking pair, but what had attracted Gabriel's attention was the way they wore their guns on their hips. It was clear just from the positioning of the weapons and the oiled leather of the belts and holsters that these two took their sidearms seriously and undoubtedly knew how to use them.

"We've got bigger things in mind," Gabriel said, although he did not—yet. Not in any detail. "This summer there's going to be more trains coming through here when they take over more from the stages. They'll move a lot of payrolls and mail."

"That sounds like something we'd be interested in," Ross said. His voice was rather broken and jerky when he spoke, the result of a nerve disease. "That right, Cassidy?"

Cassidy grunted noncommittally in an attempt to preserve his self-image in the exchange, like a

120

primary-grade kid caught in with a group of upper-class boys. "Sure. Why not?"

"I'm going to own this territory," Gabriel went on. His dark eyes bored into Cassidy's. "Maybe you know how we handle sheriffs. Well, I'm thinking on clearing them all out of this central area. I'll be the law then. We won't have to rob trains and stages then, we'll just charge them big fees for coming through here. And they'll be glad to pay it. We'll be protecting them from other robberies."

"I'll be damned," Ross said. "Who'd ever think of something like that?"

"Just me," Gabriel told him and let a crooked smile move his mouth.

"My brother here is real smart," Coot put in. "You boys don't know the half of it."

As they spoke, a big black man walked in and went over to the caged office, looking for the management. He was dressed like a cowboy and was the cook for an outfit that was droving a herd just east of town. He was very black, and he wore dungarees that had a tattered look. He wore chaps made of horsehair and had a battered, narrow-brimmed hat atop his head.

"Anybody here?" he called out toward the rear.

Coot and Cassidy turned and stared toward him, whereas Gabriel and the fellow Ross just gave the man a glance. Coot grinned and tittered. Black men had always fascinated him.

"I like your ideas," Ross was saying to Gabriel. "But I guess you'd have to be a pretty tough hombre to pull off what you're telling us."

Gabriel saw he had a point to make here. Over at the cage, the black man had turned to them. He called over. "Any of you gentlemen know where that no-good clerk is hiding? I got to buy some eggs."

Gabriel glanced at the man, then drew his Schofield .45 from its holster. "This thing seemed to shoot to the right the last time I used it at Stinking Creek," he said casually. He took careful aim as the man's eyes widened. Gabriel squeezed the trigger. The gun roared loudly in the room, and a blue hole appeared in the black fellow's forehead. His head whiplashed violently, and he crashed against the wire cage, then slid to the floor, his limbs jerking there.

"No, I guess it shoots pretty straight now," Gabriel said, sliding the gun back into its leather without looking again at the dead man. He swigged some beer as the others stared hard at the new corpse on the floor.

"Now, what was that you was saying about being tough?" he said in the low, hard voice.

Ross and Cassidy turned somber faces toward him, while Coot giggled quietly, staring at the body on the floor. A smear of blood covered a large section of the wire of the office cage.

"It—wasn't nothing," Ross said quietly. "It wasn't nothing at all."

It was just a couple of days later that Sumner rode into Bingham. In a village nearby, he had heard that a man of Lobo's description had been seen in Bingham in the company of another man. Sumner figured the other man might be Jesus Cuesta and that he and Lobo were there to join back up with the Gabriels. When Sumner arrived, therefore, he figured he just might find all four of the Gabriel gang there, and he calculated that that would mean a high-risk factor for him. All of these men were good with guns, and Lobo and Gabriel were particularly good. If he got in a situation where he had to confront most or all of them at once by himself, he realized he might not walk away from it. But the high bounties compelled him to persist. He was in need of money, and there was a lot of it on their heads.

However, it was only Billy Lobo and Cuesta that were hanging out in Bingham. They had been instructed by Gabriel to stay put there until he arrived, and they had been doing nothing but eating, drinking, and trying to keep a low profile. They could not afford to make trouble until Gabriel and Coot had rejoined them.

Billy Lobo intended to make an exception to that rule, though. He had seen a young woman on the street the day before who had caught his eye and made something move in his groin. She was unmarried and lived alone, widowed. Lobo had decided to go tonight and entertain himself with her. There was no law in Bingham to give him any trouble over it. He had planned on going to her place at seven that evening.

But Sumner rode in at three.

It was a wet April day, and it was sprinkling rain when Sumner rode in on the coal-black stallion.

Water ran off the brim of his dark hat in slow rivulets, and the horse was shiny slick with the light rain. As he walked the stallion into the muddy street, the place looked all closed up, like some of the southern towns during a siesta.

Sumner stopped in front of the Dogey Hotel and regarded it soberly. It was the only hostelry in the town, and the outlaws were probably staying there, he figured. He dismounted and tethered his mount to a rail and let the animal stand in the rain. He went up wet, slippery steps, his spurs clinking dully on the wood. He paused at the door and eased the Peacemaker in and out of its holster a couple of times. He was wearing a light-colored riding coat, below knee length, open at the front for access to the gun. He entered the hotel lobby, and it was dark in there for midday. There was no clerk about. He went to the counter in the far corner and examined the register. He found the names of Smith and Jones and figured those were Lobo and Cuesta. There was no evidence that they had been joined by Gabriel and his brother. A clerk finally showed up, and Sumner checked in under an alias, then asked about Lobo and Cuesta.

"Oh, yes, they been here a few days," the clerk said. "But they're not in now, Mr. Sloan. I heard Mr. Smith say that him and Mr. Jones was going down to have a bite to eat at the café."

Sumner nodded. "I'll bring my gear in later," he said.

"Just as you say," the clerk told him.

Sumner went back out to the street, and the rain had stopped, but there was the ominous rumbling

124

of thunder out over the plains not far from town. He stripped off the riding coat and was left with the corduroy undercoat that gave him a rather dressy look. He threw the riding coat over his saddle. The stallion shied and nickered, and he laid a hand on its nose for a moment. The animal had caught the excitement that was building inside his rider.

Sumner drew the Colt, swung the cylinder over, checked the ammunition, then slid the weapon back into its holster. If it was Lobo and Cuesta down the street in that café, it would be him or them that walked out of there. The outcome would not even have been in doubt if he had had O'Brien with him. But he had gone against more than one professional gun before and lived to tell it.

The café was called the Bingham Rose, and there were plate-glass windows which revealed the interior, which was brightly lighted with kerosene lamps because of the darkness of the day. Sumner could not see much through the glass, though, because it was steamed up some. He opened the door to the place and entered.

There were a dozen tables scattered through a sizeable room and a counter on a wall to the left, a few stools standing there. There was only one person in the room, and it was Jesus Cuesta. He sat at a table facing the door, and he looked up casually when Sumner entered. Then his face settled into a deep frown. He recognized Sumner from that night at Willard, and since then he had learned that the man he and Lobo had left with Nightshade, so that Nightshade might kill him

125

slowly and with pleasure, was Certainty Sumner.

Cuesta felt a ripple of hot excitement course through his insides. His hand went uncertainly toward his hip, and Sumner stopped him with a command.

"Just stay put." He did not have his hand anywhere near his gun, but his very reputation halted Cuesta. He let his hand move slightly away from his holster but kept it out of sight under the table's edge.

Sumner walked over to the table, looking around the room as he went. The sound of his spurs punctured the silence with each step he took. He stopped in front of the table where Cuesta sat.

"Mind if I join you?"

Cuesta relaxed some. He hesitated, then shrugged. "Why not?" he said in his Spanish accent.

Sumner carefully pulled a straight chair out and sat down on it across from Cuesta. An aroma of coffee and cooking vegetables came from the kitchen, behind swinging doors. Another doorway had a sign above it: "Gentlemen." That doorway was almost directly behind Cuesta.

"Where's your friend Billy?" Sumner said in his smooth voice.

Cuesta looked swarthy and blocky, sitting there. He looked at the place setting in front of Sumner and knew it wouldn't do much good to lie. "He's here."

"Where?"

Cuesta jerked his head. "He's in there relieving himself."

Sumner glanced at the men's room door and

126

nodded. "Nice seeing you again, Cuesta."

Cuesta licked suddenly dry lips. He knew Sumner was good. "Look, Sumner. That night at Willard. We didn't know who you were."

Sumner smiled a handsome smile. "I know. If you had, you wouldn't have left Nightshade to do the job."

Cuesta averted his gaze from Sumner's easy one. His right hand was still below the table. "You lived. One of us didn't. Why don't you let it go?" He was stalling, hoping Billy Lobo would return.

Sumner held his smile. "Even if you hadn't beat on me like you did, I'd be here. That part is business. But the beating I took makes it downright necessary."

Cuesta shrugged. He wore a heavy black mustache on his square face, and his eyes were coal black. Long red underwear showed at his shirt collar, and he had a greasy waistcoat over the shirt. "I can't argue with your artillery, Sumner. If you want to take us in, tell it to Billy. Maybe he'll just ride to the nearest sheriff with you, *compadre*. He is a reasonable fellow."

"Are you reasonable, Cuesta?" Sumner said, no longer smiling.

"Sure, *amigo*. You can ask anybody."

"What about down in Mexico, where you're a lowdown *cobarde* and mother killer?" Sumner said in a slow, deliberate tone, his aquiline face set in new, hard lines.

Cuesta's face darkened with anger. Outside, a flash of lightning brightened the sky, and then a thunderclap exploded like dynamite overhead. In that same moment, Cuesta's hand under the table went quickly to his Mauser revolver.

The movement above table level was slight, but Sumner did not miss it. In a fluid motion that dazzled the eye, he grabbed the Colt and merely turned it upward, still in its holster on his belly. The Colt banged out in the room, and hot lead bit into Cuesta's abdomen below the tabletop. The Mexican's own gun then went off, and splintered wood in the floor beside Sumner's left foot, while Cuesta went crashing down with his chair, taking his empty china plate and a fork with him, his eyes wide in sudden pain and terror.

In the next instant, Billy Lobo appeared in the doorway of the service room, looking mean eyed. He spotted Sumner first, then Cuesta, who lay in a pool of his own blood. Lobo stepped slowly out into the room, about twenty feet from Sumner. In the following moment of silence, the waiter came into the room saucer eyed, holding a tray with a couple of steaming bowls of food on it. He looked at Cuesta on the floor and dropped the tray. It crashed to the floor, making a big racket. Neither Sumner nor Lobo looked toward him. He hesitated, then turned and hurried out of the room, grunting.

Sumner stood slowly and moved away from the table.

"It's you, you sonofabitch!" Billy Lobo hissed out at him.

"It's me," Sumner said. He was tightening some inside. Lobo was probably as fast as anybody in the territory, he knew.

"We don't have to do this," Lobo said warningly. "You can still walk out of here alive, bounty hunter. That Willard thing ain't nothing to hold a grudge over."

"It's not really Willard," Sumner told him. "It's mainly business, Billy." He lowered his voice. "You're just too valuable to me dead."

He saw Lobo's face go straight. "You're as brash as a flour peddler running for governor, mister. And kind of reckless, too. I reckon I can shade you."

"I can't hear you when you talk like that," Sumner said quietly.

"They tell me you can hear a man's arm swinging in its socket at a hundred yards in a windstorm," Lobo replied.

Sumner grunted. "They tell me you're so fast you can draw and fire three times in the tick of a wall clock," he countered. "Why don't we find out if that's just prairie fog?"

Lobo's jaw muscles tightened in his lean, bony face, and he moved his feet slightly apart and let his gunhand hang free over the holster of his Joslyn .44. "Why don't we?" he said in a low growl.

Sumner waited until he saw the subtle change in Lobo's eyes and the uncocking of the fingers of Lob's right hand, and then they were both slapping leather.

Billy Lobo's draw was so fast that it appeared the Joslyn had jumped into his hand like a snake. Sumner's Colt came up at about the same time, but Lobo beat him by a fraction of a second. His gun blasted in the silence and hit Sumner in the rib cage at his side, the shot off its mark. Sumner's Colt had already fired, though, and the bullet struck Billy Lobo in the heart violently, as if he had been hit by a lightning bolt from the sky outside.

Sumner went twisting backwards and crashed through the plate-glass window behind him and hit on the boardwalk outside. Lobo flew against the wall like a rocket mortar at Fort McHenry, his heart bursting open inside him and making a smear on the wall there out of proportion to the hole in his torso from front to back. He stood there for a moment then, looking down at his chest as if tarantula bitten, then toppled to the floor on his side.

Sumner, out in a renewed rain again, rose slowly and stood. The Colt still hung in his right hand, like an extension of that appendage. He looked down at his side, under his coat, and saw the blood. Lobo's shot had cut through flesh there and chipped a rib. He touched it and grimaced; he felt faint.

He had lost his hat, and his dark hair hung sticky wet onto his forehead. He holstered the Peacemaker and reentered the café through its door, holding his side.

The waiter was there again, staring at the carnage. Sumner regarded Lobo's figure solemnly and then looked down at the inert Cuesta. He figured they were both dead. He looked over at the waiter.

"I want you as a witness," he said, breathing hard.

"Huh?" the other man said, looking very scared.

"These men are Billy Lobo and Jesus Cuesta. I killed them in self-defense for the bounties on them. My name is Sumner. I want you to remember that. For the law."

The fellow nodded slowly. "You're Certainty Sumner?"

"That's right."

"Okay. I'll remember."

"You got a doctor here?"

"We got a vet," the waiter said hollowly. "Down the street a few doors."

Sumner nodded wearily. "I'll be back for them," he said. He reached into a pocket and threw a gold coin onto a table. "Take care of them for me. Get them into a back room or something."

The fellow nodded his agreement. "All right, Sumner."

Sumner turned and left the place again. Walking painfully down the street in the rain, he felt very lucky to be alive.

He had survived another day in his business.

Now there was Luther Gabriel.

Chapter Seven

The news about Aaron Seger and Annie had sat hard with O'Brien. He had just holed up in Duran for several days after Sumner left and drank hard at the saloon. Garrett was gone, too, and O'Brien was glad. He didn't want anybody around to jaw with him. He wanted only to sit and recall those early days in the hills of Tennessee, when men like his father and Seger stood tall in their valley because they could put meat on the table and because their word meant something.

When the drinking was finished, though, O'Brien went into the general store with his .38 calibre Dardick 1500 revolver and laid it on the counter before the slick-haired, jowly proprietor.

"How much will you give me for that in a trade for a shotgun?" he asked in his deep voice. He made no effort to intimidate people, but his mere proximity across the counter made the proprietor wary, that and his rough manner.

The fellow picked up the Dardick and looked it

over. It was flawlessly kept and a very nice sidearm. He looked up at O'Brien.

"What kind of shotgun you want, hunter?"

O'Brien glanced at a shelf behind the owner, where several kinds of guns hung. "Let me see that Remington ten gauge there."

The proprietor took the gun down and handed it to O'Brien. O'Brien took it and turned it over in his big hands. It was a handsome gun with double barrels and triggers, and a walnut stock. "I like this," O'Brien told him. "What kind of deal can you make me?"

The other man thought a moment. "You sure you want to get rid of that Dardick? That's a well-balanced, straight-shooting pistol."

O'Brien looked down at it. He didn't really need it for hunting. And for going after men, he did not take to quick draws with peashooters. It just wasn't his style. It did not fit his character.

"I'm sure," he said. "Now, can we talk business?"

The owner shrugged. "Yes, I like the Dardick. A double eagle and the revolver, and the shotgun is yours."

O'Brien nodded. "It's a bargain." He reached into a pouch and took out two gold coins and laid them on the counter, and the proprietor put the Dardick on a shelf. O'Brien hefted the gun and looked up.

"You got a hacksaw somewhere I can use?"

The man frowned. "I think so."

"Let me borrow it for a bit."

The fellow hunched thick shoulders. "Come with me."

He took O'Brien into a storeroom, found a saw, and gave it to O'Brien. O'Brien laid the gun across two sawhorses, and made a mark across both barrels about a foot and a half from the trigger assembly. Then he set the saw onto the barrels.

"Hey, you aren't going to mutilate that beautiful gun?" the owner said.

O'Brien glanced over at him, then began sawing along the line he had made. "I don't need long-distance accuracy for my purpose. I need destructive power."

"Just what is your purpose?" the proprietor asked.

O'Brien was biting into the metal with the saw. It was tough work, by hand, but O'Brien had done it before. He stopped and gave the other man a hard look.

"Well, it's none of my business," the owner said softly.

In just a short time, O'Brien had cut through both barrels, and then he took a file to the edges until they were smooth. He hefted the gun and was satisfied that it also had better balance. "I think that will do it," he said.

"You lost your front sight," the owner told him.

"I don't need sights," O'Brien said. "Now let's go find me a couple pouches of shells."

O'Brien went out to his Appaloosa while the proprietor got some ammunition for the gun. O'Brien undid the bedroll behind his saddle and rolled the gun up in it. The other long guns were in saddle scabbards on either side of the horse. Now the only small weapon O'Brien owned was the hunting knife he wore in his right boot.

The owner came out into the street on that sunny, cool morning and delivered the ammunition to O'Brien, who stuffed it into a saddle wallet. The owner looked again at the size and wild appearance of the buffalo hunter and licked his lips before he spoke.

"You aren't . . . figuring on using that thing around here? Are you?"

O'Brien gave him a rather somber grin and boarded the big stallion. "Don't worry, mister. I'm heading out right now."

The other man breathed easier. "Well. Good luck to you, whatever you're after."

O'Brien nodded. "A man can always use some," he said.

Back at Bingham, things had taken an unexpected turn for Sumner. When he had returned to the café to collect the bodies of Billy Lobo and Jesus Cuesta, he found out that he had only one corpse. He had come back with his side bandaged, in a lot of pain, and was very unhappy when the waiter reported to him, "I dragged that Lobo fellow out of sight, into a closet in back of the place. It took me a while to situate him, and when I came back, the other fellow was gone. The one you called Cuesta."

"Gone?" Sumner had been very angry.

"There was some blood up by the front door. I think he's still alive, Sumner. He must have got away."

"Sonofabitch. I thought he might be hit wide."

"Maybe he crawled off to die somewhere else."

"No. It was my mistake. I should have finished him off. I was already thinking about Lobo."

"I'll go check around town. Maybe somebody saw him."

But it was too late. Cuesta's mount was gone, and Sumner realized he had finished only one of the Gabriel gang, not two. Actually, the prize on Lobo was twice that on Cuesta, but Sumner had already been counting on both bounties. He was running low on finances and needed the cash to meet expenses in his hunt for Gabriel himself.

The waiter had been correct in his assessment of what had happened. Cuesta had come around about the time Sumner left the place, and had felt his gut to learn that the hot slug from Sumner's gun had passed through him up near his appendix, just under his diaphragm, without ripping him up much. He knew that if he could get to a doctor, he would live. He had crawled out the front door and into the rain, hiding under the porch out there in the mud and water, still bleeding from front and back. He had still been there when Sumner returned, but while Sumner was inside, he had gotten out of his cover and to his feet, and had stumbled to the livery nearby, somehow mounting his horse and riding off. He had headed for a nearby village where he got lucky and found a visiting doctor. That fellow had performed some surgery on him at gunpoint. Then Cuesta had sent a wire off to Gabriel in Magdalena, telling him what had happened.

Sumner, meanwhile, was holing up in Bingham. He had to heal from his own wound, and he had to go through some red tape to receive the reward money on Lobo. He had gotten hold of a traveling photographer, and the morning after the shooting, Sumner had sat Billy Lobo up on a chair outside the café, and the picture taker had set up his tripod camera and hidden himself under a cape to focus in on the stripped-to-the-waist corpse with the blue hole in its chest.

But that was only for additional proof, if the governor's office gave him any trouble. He had already sent a wire, attesting to the facts of Billy's death and giving his witness's name.

Sumner was down, despite his success with Lobo. He was in a lot of discomfort from his healing side wound, and it was still bothering him that Cuesta had eluded death and was still out there somewhere, reporting back to Gabriel and making more trouble.

The albumen photograph of Billy Lobo was the only one ever taken of the outlaw, and somehow he achieved a look of closed-eyes dignity in that picture that had forever escaped him in real life. Later, it would be circulated in bars and public places, and Sumner's reputation would soar again, and people would quit talking about how Sumner had killed Curly Quentin and would begin tall tales about the shootout between Certainty Sumner and Billy Lobo without having the slightest notion of what had actually happened there in Bingham.

Now, just a couple of days after O'Brien's

purchase of the Remington shotgun in Duran, Luther Gabriel was still dealing with the news that Certainty Sumner had killed Billy Lobo and badly wounded one of Gabriel's most trusted subordinates, Cuesta. Even though Lobo had been the fastest and perhaps most dangerous of Gabriel's hirelings, he had been entirely unpredictable and his only skill had been with his gun. On the other hand, Jesus Cuesta could keep accounts, shoe a horse, and blow a safe. He often had ideas about proposed robberies of which Gabriel had never thought. Consequently, Gabriel was more concerned about Cuesta's recovery than he was about the loss of Lobo.

It was several days after the news that they were all sitting around a rented room on the second floor of a rooming house, Gabriel, Coot, and the two new men, when Gabriel first discussed the matter in detail with all of them.

Coot was propped up on a double bed, cleaning his Wells Fargo revolver, and seeming to pay little attention to the conversation. Ross and Cassidy, the newcomers who had gained a sudden respect for Gabriel when he had gunned down the unfortunate man in the gambling hall, sat on straight chairs across the room from each other. Cassidy was paring his nails with a razor-sharp penknife, and the older Ross had his chair tipped back against the wall, watching Gabriel. Gabriel was standing over beside a window where the sun came in and backlighted him, so that his harsh features were softened some. His arms were crossed, and a somber look secured itself firmly on

138

his rough features.

"That was a bit of bad luck at Bingham," he was saying to them. "That sonofabitch Sumner must have sneaked up on them two; he could never have killed Billy in a drawdown."

The hawk-nosed Ross looked up at him. "If you're talking about Certainty Sumner, ain't he the one that killed Curly Quentin?"

"That's him," Coot said, without looking up from his work. He slid a rod through the barrel of the revolver and worked it back and forth there. "If I ever get that whore's son in my sights, like Cuesta done at Willard, I'll blow his goddam head off."

Young Cassidy in his ill-fitting clothes turned red-rimmed eyes toward Ross and caught his look and grinned. Ross did not return the grin, afraid that Gabriel might take offense.

"Let's hope he comes here," Ross said in his jerky voice. "We'll kill him any way we have to."

"I'm not worried over no goddam back-shooting bounty hunter," Gabriel growled. "But he put us back a little. We don't just need capital to run this territory, we need guns. Now I've got another recruiting job ahead of me."

"We know a fellow in Albuquerque that might come in," Cassidy told him. "Remember Walcott, Ross?"

Ross nodded. "Used to be a sheriff over in Arizona Territory. Till they fired him for back-shooting a cowpoke that he owed some money." Now he grinned.

"Hell, we don't need no lawman in with us," Coot said in his high voice.

"Shut up, damn it!" Gabriel said harshly. He caught Coot's eye with a look that most men would have gone pale under. He turned back to Ross. "I'll give that some thought. In the meantime, though, I'm going to Cuesta. He's holed up trying to heal in a place near Bingham. If that bastard of a bounty man is there, I'll kill him. Then I'll bring Cuesta back here. It will take him a while to heal, so we'll just have to go easy."

"Brother Luther's killed four or five bounty hunters," Coot said blithely, then looked up quickly to see if he had offended Gabriel.

Gabriel just looked hard at him.

"When will you be leaving for Bingham?" Ross said.

"I'm going later today. Cuesta needs help," Gabriel said.

"I'd be happy to ride along," Ross said. "In case there's trouble down there."

"There won't be no trouble," Gabriel said. "It's just as well you and Cassidy ain't seen with me a lot just yet."

Coot had put the gun down. "I'm getting bored, Luther. Why do we got to wait for Cuesta? Let's get to setting this territory on its ear."

Gabriel shook his head. "You got mustard seed for brains, little brother. You don't just go off half-cocked on something this big."

"I sure would like to get my knife on that bounty hunter," Coot said wistfully.

Ross narrowed his eyes on Coot and glanced at Cassidy.

Gabriel shoved himself off from the wall. He

140

looked very tough and dangerous in the black beard and scowl. His Schofield .45 hung menacingly on his hip in a low-slung holster.

"I'll be riding out now." He glanced at Coot and then back toward Ross. "I want you all to lay low. I don't need any trouble back here while I'm gone. I'll be back in a few days, and I want it all quiet hereabouts. You take my meaning?"

"I understand," Ross said.

"When we get Cuesta back here, then we're going to start standing this territory on its ear, but I want peace and tranquillity till then."

"Goddam boring town," Coot grumbled.

Gabriel looked over at him for a long moment and wondered whether to take him along, just to keep him out of trouble. But he decided this was a one-man job. "I'll be back in a few days," he finally said.

Then he turned and left.

It was the very next day that O'Brien got a lead on the Gabriels at the same time that Certainty Sumner was finally leaving Bingham and heading out in the wrong direction in his quest for Luther Gabriel.

Sumner calculated incorrectly that Cuesta had headed southeast out of Bingham, because it was a less populated area in that direction, and he figured Cuesta would find hiding out easier down that way. In fact, Cuesta had cunningly figured Sumner would come to that conclusion and had holed up in a small village just west of Bingham, between that town and Socorro. He had found a vacated cabin there and had just squatted in it, waiting for Gabriel. He had lost a lot of blood. Despite his being sewed up by a drunken traveling doctor, he was in bad shape. It would be weeks before he was any use to Gabriel, but he had made the whole thing sound more optimistic to Gabriel in the two wires he had gotten out from Bingham through a boy messenger. He figured Gabriel would not come and get him if he sounded bad, and he was right.

Sumner had figured if he could locate Cuesta, Cuesta could lead him to Gabriel. That much was right, but his beginning search was off the mark.

O'Brien, though, not even knowing Sumner had been in a confrontation with Cuesta and Lobo, nor that Sumner was only a day's ride away, had run onto some good luck in his own hunt. He was out on the trail, heading toward Soccoro, when he came upon another rider, heading in the opposite direction. The fellow reined in on his mount when he saw O'Brien, and O'Brien spurred the Appaloosa on up to him.

It was one of those primordial spring mornings that stir the blood and renew man's awareness of his closeness to the rich earth. It had rained the night before, and the ground was damp, increasing the redolence from budding wildflowers. Through the early morning O'Brien had ridden at a steady pace, hunkered in his saddle, hoping he was not up a dead end in his hunt. He had rather enjoyed the ride, considering the circumstances. He had skirted a ranch where a scattering of longhorns had drifted up against a low range of buttes, the nearer ones standing knee deep in a tula bed. Later on, meandering down a draw, he had seen blooming catclaw and prickly pear, and some granjeno and huisache. Mesquite trees and cottonwoods were getting green already and also the wild pear. O'Brien had been through this country before, on the hunt for shaggies, and remembered it well. He had made hardship camp all over this territory, cooking in a tin can and sleeping with his Winchester beside his bedroll. It was his kind of life. Towns had become almost like prisons to him. He sometimes felt suffocated there.

"Morning, stranger," the other rider said to O'Brien.

O'Brien nodded, looking the other man over. When you met another rider out on the trail, you first assessed whether he was any immediate danger to you before your guard was relaxed. This stranger was rather small and dumpy and middle-aged, and wore Eastern clothing with a dapper, narrow-brimmed hat. He had a rather large suitcase affixed to his dun mare's rump, behind his saddle, where a bedroll would ordinarily have gone. O'Brien took him for a drummer of some kind or a gambler.

He did not wear a gun, at least not one that was visible.

"Where you coming from?" O'Brien asked.

"Just rode out from Socorro," the fellow replied. "Been selling Bibles to the squatters and sharecroppers thereabouts. Name is Funk. Can I sell you a Good Book, mister?"

O'Brien had never learned to read much, but he was not about to tell this stranger that. "My Daddy read the whole thing through to me when I was a tadpole," he said. "I suspect once past it is enough."

Funk took a metal flask from an inside pocket, screwed a cap off, and took a long swallow of the whiskey inside. He proffered the flask to O'Brien. "This will warm your guts on a cool morning."

O'Brien hesitated, then shook his shaggy head. "Much obliged."

"I got religious tracts, too. They praise the glorious word of the Lord, mister. I can let you have one gratis, if you're of a mind." He was replacing the flask to its hiding place.

The Appaloosa nickered quietly, and O'Brien moved slightly on his saddle, making the leather squeak under his weight. The sharp aroma of alcohol insinuated its way past him and polluted the crisp air for a moment. "Is there any law in Socorro nowadays?" he said, ignoring the second offer of literature.

"No, sir. They ain't hired a sheriff since that outlaw killed their other one about a year ago. You know, that one they call Gabriel."

O'Brien's eyes squinted down. "Gabriel killed their sheriff?"

Funk nodded. "Done it slow, too, I hear. That scared anybody else off. This whole territory is afraid of that demon from hell, mister. I hear talk he'll run it some day. It's a godless, lawless land, and I'll be glad when I'm through it."

"Hmmph," O'Brien said.

144

"I talked to a fellow yesterday, said he saw that bunch back in Magdalena. I'm praising the Lord I'm not headed in that direction."

"Did he say how long ago they were there?" O'Brien asked.

Funk shrugged. "No. Couldn't been long, though. This fellow just come from there."

O'Brien remembered how Aaron Seger had died and saw the note from Annie to him in that neat longhand style of hers, and his insides tightened up again. Two nights ago, out on the trail, he had had a dream. He was out hunting shaggies and had come upon the white buffalo, and a man was riding it, and the man was Luther Gabriel. Gabriel and the buffalo were charging O'Brien, and the animal was big as a house, and Gabriel was firing two revolvers at O'Brien as they came, and O'Brien could see evil red eyes in both the buffalo and Gabriel, and as they came closer and loomed over O'Brien, he saw that Gabriel and the buffalo were one animal with Gabriel's torso growing out of the shaggy's white back. Then, just as O'Brien was about to be trampled under enormous hooves, he woke up in a cold sweat.

"Hey," Funk said. "You ain't one of them, are you? Cause if you are, I don't mean no offense. Live and let live, I say. Who am I to judge another man. The Scriptures tell you—"

O'Brien spurred the Appaloosa, nodded, and rode on past without another word. The drummer stopped in mid-sentence and just stared after him for a long moment, watching O'Brien's broad back recede into the distance, and feeling more

145

comfortable as the distance lengthened between them.

"May the Lord watch over you in your journey!" he called out after the buffalo hunter. Then he turned back and spurred his own mount. "Queer kind of bird," he said to himself and rode on down the trail in the opposite direction from O'Brien.

When O'Brien passed through Socorro later that morning, he was only a couple hours ride from where Luther Gabriel was heading in the other direction looking for Jesus Cuesta, but O'Brien would never know that. His information put the whole gang in Magdalena, and that was where O'Brien was now riding.

O'Brien had no thought of making a citizen's arrest of any of the Gabriel gang when he caught up with them. He had even less regard for the niceties of the law than Sumner. When a dog went rabid, a man shot it. And O'Brien figured that Gabriel and his kind warranted less respect than any gone-crazy dog.

O'Brien arrived in Magdalena the next afternoon. It was a lazy, spring day, and the town was soft-buzzingly quiet. There was the occasional hum of bumble bees on the honey-sweet air and the irregular passage of horse and buggy clop-clopping and squeaking down the main street. O'Brien reined up before the gambling hall where Gabriel and Coot had met up with the newcomers Ross and Cassidy a while ago. He read the sign that said, "Magdalena Gaming," as he tethered the tired Appaloosa to the hitching rail. This was the kind of place he might find the Gabriels, he figured. He undid the sawed-off Remington ten gauge from his mount's irons, loaded it, and climbed the steps to the entrance.

Coot and the two new men were in Magdalena, all right, waiting for the return of Luther Gabriel with Cuesta. But they were not in the gambling hall when O'Brien walked in.

"Sure, three of them was here earlier," the clerk told him when he inquired. He was by now terrified of the gang and was eyeing O'Brien fearfully, too. "They friends of yours?"

O'Brien was getting tired of being asked that particular question. "Three?" he said.

"Yes, that younger Gabriel and their new— associates," the clerk told him. He still wore the green eyeshade and sleeve garters, and his thin face held a wary look now. "I haven't seen the older Gabriel for a couple of days. I think he rode out on business."

"How long ago were the three in here?" O'Brien said, mentally calculating the odds in his head as he spoke. Not the three-to-one physical odds, but the chances of survival in a fight with at least three guns against one. There were bettors in Albuquerque who would place them pretty high against him, he knew, maybe fifty to one.

"Oh, maybe two hours."

"You know where they were heading?"

O'Brien did not sound like a friend of the outlaws now, and the clerk did not want to get into trouble with them. "You're asking a lot of questions, mister, about something that's none of my business."

O'Brien made a face. He had absolutely no patience with townspeople. He reached across the opening in the wire cage with his big left hand, grabbed the clerk by the shirt front, jerked him off his feet and pulled his head through the wire opening.

The fellow's eyes bulged as his visor fell off and his shirt front knotted up in O'Brien's fist. His chest and abdomen had been yanked up onto the counter at the window, and his shoulders were jammed tight up against the wire on the far side of it.

"Now let me ask you again," O'Brien growled. Three customers, seeing the action, stared but made no movement. "Where were they heading when they left here?"

The clerk was gasping audibly. "I heard—the one called Coot—say they ought to go out to the school."

"The school?" O'Brien said.

"There's a school marm out there. This Coot saw her one day on the street. School's out today, so he—suggested they go out there and—entertain themselves with her."

O'Brien was still staring hard into the clerk's face, and the clerk could smell the faint odor of buffalo on him. "Where's the school?"

"Right straight out on this street to the east. About a half-mile from town."

O'Brien released his hold on the other fellow, and he slid back through the opening, grabbing onto the counter, breathing irregularly. "Please. Don't tell them I sent you."

O'Brien grunted. "I don't reckon there'll be much talking," he said in a deep, low voice. Then he turned and left.

At about that same time, out at the Magdalena primary school, Coot and the two new men were enjoying themselves. They had found the young teacher by herself in the school building working on some papers and had begun harassing her immediately. She had thought at first that she could get rid of them by speaking harshly to them, but then she became very frightened when it was apparent what kind of men they were. They now surrounded her at her desk, and Ross had asked her for a kiss, and she had asked them again to leave.

"Please," she was saying to them. She was a rather attractive young woman in her early thirties, a divorcée from Kansas City who had come farther west to make a new life for herself. She had met a store proprietor in Magdalena who liked her a lot, and she thought he was about ready to ask her to marry him. Her stay in Magdalena had been a very positive experience until this moment. "Just leave and let me be. I don't want any trouble."

"Did you hear that, boys?" Coot grinned. "She don't want no trouble."

"You already got trouble, little girl," Ross said to her.

Young Cassidy took his dirty vest off slowly. "Let's not talk about it no more," he said in a low voice. "I'm going to do things to this little lady she'll be talking about the rest of her natural days. Look at the milk breasts on her and them wide hips. She can service all of us and then some."

"No, please!" she muttered.

Coot was very close to her. He remembered the sweet young flesh of Annie Seger, and his lust got hold of him. He reached out toward her, and she backed up against a blackboard behind her. He put a hand on her left breast, and she gasped and knocked it away, and he grinned more widely. "Mmm, that's mighty soft," he said. "Let's see what all them curves look like under that gingham."

"I'm for that," Ross said quietly.

"I want to see what it's like up between them legs," Cassidy said. "I bet it's mighty hot up there under all that cloth."

"You're going to do it for all of us, missy," Coot grinned. "And you're going to do a little bit of everything."

"Oh, God," the teacher said in a low, croaking voice.

Suddenly Coot reached again and caught the neck of the blue gingham dress, yanking hard on it. With a loud ripping sound, it tore down toward her waist. Some underclothing came with it, and her left breast was partially bared. She began screaming then, and Cassidy backhanded her across the face and cut her screaming off. She began sobbing quietly as Cassidy put a hand on the bare flesh. Then they all heard the clinking of spurs in the open doorway behind them.

They turned, one by one, and saw O'Brien standing there.

The buffalo man filled the doorway with his

presence. Backlighted by afternoon sun, he looked even bigger and more ominous than usual. The shotgun hung from his right hand loosely, and the sun cast his shadow clear across the floor and the small desks that separated him from the men at the blackboard.

O'Brien had known he had located them when he found their horses outside. He had prepared himself for a showdown. His only interest was in Luther Gabriel and his brother Coot, for what they had done in Stinking Creek. But he knew he would have to deal with these new allies of theirs. He stood there now looking at the scene before him, realizing he had arrived just in time for the schoolteacher.

"Butt out, mister. This here is a private party," Ross said harshly to O'Brien.

The teacher held her hands over her breasts and focused on O'Brien. "Help me!" she muttered pitifully.

Cassidy turned to square off at O'Brien. "Make tracks, hunter," he growled. "And forget what you saw here or you're a dead man."

Coot had not really given O'Brien a good look until Cassidy identified him as a hunter, because of the rawhides and the long gun. Coot now turned fully toward O'Brien and squinted down at him, recalling that it had been a buffalo hunter named O'Brien who had killed Nightshade. He quickly looked outside through a window to see if Sumner was with him and satisfied himself that this man who must be O'Brien was alone.

"Which one of you sacks of mule shit is Coot

Gabriel?" came O'Brien's low, hard response.

Ross and Cassidy both grew quick scowls on their faces. Cassidy's hand went out over the revolver on his hip. "You got a foul mouth, hunter. Maybe I'll have to clean it up for you."

"I'm Coot Gabriel," Coot's high voice came then, kind of whispery and uneven. He figured O'Brien had teamed up with Sumner for bounties. He had no reason to believe that O'Brien's motive for being there was revenge.

O'Brien narrowed deep blue eyes on him. "I guess that would be the Coot Gabriel that murdered Aaron Seger in Stinking Creek and raped his daughter?"

The teacher gasped softly.

All three gunmen were facing O'Brien down now. Coot had found some courage, seeing O'Brien had only a shotgun and realizing that that would have to go against three guns.

"What's that got to do with you, hunter?" Coot said with a bit more arrogance in his thin voice.

O'Brien glanced at the woman. "Ma'am, you better get out of here," he said in a low monotone.

Ross scowled angrily. "The hell she will!" he said.

Coot glanced at her. "Let her go," he said.

"Hell, let's take the hunter and then her!" Cassidy said loudly.

But Coot wanted himself and Gabriel to be rid of this big man in the doorway, and he wanted their efforts concentrated on that alone. *I said, let her go!"* he yelled in a high-pitched scream.

Ross and Cassidy looked over at his wild face

and then at each other. Cassidy reluctantly stepped away from the young woman, and she hurried past them and to a far wall, where she opened a second door and slid through it to a back room which she passed through to the outside beyond.

Coot took a couple of steps forward. He stood on one side of the desk, Cassidy on the other. Ross was positioned behind it, but it gave him no cover except for his legs.

"Didn't know you had nothing to do with the Segers, mister," Coot said now. "But that's the way it goes. I'll tell you one thing. That kid was one sugary little piece of female flesh. Of course, I reckon you know that already."

O'Brien felt the raw anger flush up into his face. He walked over to a place where an aisle between the small desks gave him a clear shot at all three gunmen, his spurs making metallic insults to the deathly silence.

"You're a yellow, rancid piece of dung," O'Brien growled in a hard-as-iron half-whisper.

Coot felt the excitement of the moment take control of him. He felt it in his chest, his face, his fingertips. "Take him!" he blurted out to the others.

It was Ross who drew first in response to Coot's barked command. He went for a long-barreled revolver at his side as O'Brien raised the muzzle of the shotgun, falling into a deep crouch. The big gun and the sidearm went off almost simultaneously, and O'Brien felt a hot tugging at his left arm as the lead ripped shallowly into flesh there. At the same moment, the shot from the Remington ten gauge chipped splinters out of the teacher's desk, peppered holes into the blackboard behind Ross, and tore his midsection to pieces, almost cutting him in half.

Ross hit the blackboard hard, and blood and pieces of flesh dripped down its surface. He hung there for a moment, wide-eyed, and his gun fired into the floor. He then slid to his knees, his torso in one direction and his legs and hips in the other.

Coot and Cassidy hesitated only a split second, then were both firing at O'Brien. Coot's Wells Fargo barked out its message first, and the shot creased O'Brien's side under the rawhides as he dived forward in the aisle on its right side and then rolled left as he had done so often in a stampede to avoid the hooves of buffalo or horses. Cassidy fired twice during this action, and both shots chipped up wood off the floor, the last missing O'Brien's head by an inch. Then O'Brien was re-aiming from a position on his left side, lying on the hard floor. The big gun boomed out again. Cassidy turned his head to move to his right, and the buckshot blew his face off. He went flying backwards and hit Coot, and Coot got a look inside Cassidy's faceless head as it went past. Then Cassidy also hit the blackboard, limbs jerking wildly, bits of his bone, flesh, and gray matter sticking on the dark surface beside Ross's. When he hit the floor near Coot, the arms were jerking about fitfully, and the left hand seemed to point toward O'Brien for a half moment, as if to warn Coot that the hunter was still alive.

Coot was very scared now, but he figured

O'Brien had shot himself out of ammunition. He stepped around the desk and aimed down the aisle at O'Brien's head. O'Brien, though, had drawn the hunting knife from his right boot, and, as soon as he saw Coot's figure appear at the head of the aisle, he hurled the knife sidearm in Coot's direction. The big knife turned over twice in its flight and bit Coot in the low chest like a rattlesnake, burying itself there to the hilt.

Coot's eyes saucered, and his gun went off again, tearing up the oak of a small desk top beside O'Brien's head. Coot took two steps backward and fell onto his back on the teacher's desk.

O'Brien rose slowly, hurting in his arm and ribs. On his feet, he reloaded the Remington, just in case. Then he moved up to the raised platform on which the big desk sat and stepped up there. He looked at the two others, and they were very dead. Coot was still alive, but was in bad shape. O'Brien came over and pulled the knife out of him, and Coot jerked when the steel came out.

O'Brien set the shotgun down against the desk and transferred the knife to his right hand. "I hear tell you cut Aaron up some when you killed him." O'Brien's voice came to Coot.

Coot opened his mouth to speak but could not. Blood trickled stickily through the fingers of the hand he held over the knife wound.

"Don't," Coot finally managed when he saw the big blade O'Brien held over his face. "Luther will find you and—"

O'Brien had done it only once before, to a Choctaw who had skinned another hunter alive.

But now it seemed appropriate. He grabbed Coot by the stringy hair, made an incision across Coot's forehead and around his head, and pulled the scalp off. It came in a ripping sound and was accompanied by Coot's brief scream. The scream ended in a muffled, gargling sound, and then Coot died there on the desk, his bloody skull exposed brightly to the slanting sun.

O'Brien stuck the scalp into his belt, and it stained his rawhides there. He cleaned the knife blade on Coot's shirt, then returned it to his boot. He picked up the shotgun and looked around for a moment at the carnage. Blood stained his rawhides on the left arm and wormed down his side under his clothing. He ignored it.

"I'm going to nail your goddam scalp to the door at that gambling hall," he said to the corpse on the desk. "I want it to be the first thing that brother of yours sees when he rides back into town. Then I'll kill him, too."

A moment later, O'Brien rode back into Magdalena.

Chapter Eight

Luther Gabriel, though, did not return to Magdalena.

Two days after O'Brien's vengeful shootout with Coot and Gabriel's new hirelings as Gabriel and Cuesta came back through Bingham on their way to Magdalena, Gabriel heard the news of the killings from a drifter who had just ridden through Magdalena. When Gabriel had heard the whole story and learned that Coot's scalp had hung up outside the gaming hall after the massacre, finding out the whole thing was done by the buffalo hunter who had killed Nightshade, he was not fit to be around for a couple of days. From the same drifter, he learned that O'Brien had known Aaron Seger, and Gabriel finally understood what O'Brien was up to. It was not money with him, as it was with Certainty Sumner. It went deeper than that.

Gabriel vowed, sitting there in the saloon in Bingham, that O'Brien had to die. He figured

Sumner and O'Brien were in league together, and Gabriel would give them what they wanted. He would let them find him, all right, but not at a time and place favorable to them. He would leave the area for the time being, and he would gather forces around him, and he would come back. Then he would hunt down the hunters. And they would be sorry they had ever heard of Luther Gabriel. Nobody killed kinfolk of Gabriel and lived to tell about it.

That lesson would have to be taught once again.

O'Brien hung around Magdalena for almost a week, waiting for Gabriel to return, but he finally realized the outlaw was not coming back. He then left town with Coot's scalp still decorating the gambling hall exterior. The piece of human debris was hurriedly removed when they were sure he was gone, and everybody sighed a sigh of great relief. They were more scared of O'Brien than they had been of the three gunmen. Nobody had come to O'Brien to thank him for gunning down some of the worst outlaws that area had ever seen. They looked upon him as a wild man, more savage than civilized, and the whole town kept out of his way. The teacher was going to find O'Brien and thank him for saving her life, but when it got around about the scalping, her future husband talked her out of it. She would always remember, though, the feeling of relief that coursed through her when that big figure in the doorway commanded the gunmen, indirectly, to release her.

O'Brien had no idea where to find Luther Gabriel. He rode off to Willard finally, asking questions and gathering information. One day he was sitting in Willard's run-down saloon, realizing he was getting almost nowhere in his hunt for Gabriel and recalling his first encounter with Certainty Sumner there, when Sumner walked in and came over to his table.

"Well, I'll be damned," Sumner said when he arrived beside O'Brien.

O'Brien grinned up at him. "How are they hanging, bounty hunter?"

Sumner grunted. He did not have quite the suave, poised look he had always exhibited previously. He had discarded the cravat at his throat, and his coat and vest appeared slightly wrinkled. Underneath the fit of the black hat, his dark hair was somewhat rumpled. O'Brien liked the looks of him better.

"I haven't fallen out of the saddle recently," Sumner said, returning the grin. He glanced at the bottle of whiskey sitting on the table before O'Brien. "Mind if I join you?"

O'Brien jerked his shaggy head toward a chair. "Suit yourself, Sumner. I got plenty of rot-gut here for both of us." As Sumner drew up the chair, O'Brien noted the way the heavy-looking Peacemaker stood out boldly on Sumner's flat belly, casting its ominous shadow into the room like a whispered threat. Sumner was a dangerous and deadly presence for any man who had a price on his head, O'Brien realized, and was probably as skilled a hunter in his own way as O'Brien.

O'Brien shoved an unused shot glass at him. He, himself, had been drinking from the bottle. "Here.

Pour yourself some poison."

Sumner did, then he sat there looking at it for a moment. "Did you go after Gabriel?" he finally said.

O'Brien nodded. "Did you?"

"Yes." He made a face and rubbed his side briefly. He was still changing bandages on the flesh wound under his shirt. O'Brien had a similar bandage over a wound on his rib cage and a lesser one on his left arm, and his wounds were fresher than Sumner's. But O'Brien hardly knew they were there. He was a man who felt little pain.

"Did you find him?" O'Brien asked.

"No. Did you?"

O'Brien hesitated, then shook his head. "No."

Sumner broke into a grin, and so did the buffalo hunter. Then they were both laughing softly, suddenly enjoying each other's company, and Sumner realized he had climbed over a high mountain in winning O'Brien's confidence.

Sumner swigged the whiskey in one gulp and set the glass down. "I found Billy Lobo and Cuesta at Bingham. I killed Lobo."

O'Brien nodded. "Good."

"I thought I had sent both of those bastards to hell," Sumner went on, "but that sonofabitch Cuesta crawled off like a gut-shot dog and disappeared on me. I figure he's still alive."

O'Brien hesitated, then looked over at Sumner. "I caught up with that retard brother in Magdalena. Him and a couple of dung heaps with him was getting ready to peel a school marm there like a ripe plum. I killed them."

160

He had said it in a matter-of-fact tone that impressed Sumner. When he finished the last statement, O'Brien took a long swig from the bottle.

"All of them?" Sumner said. He had heard that Gabriel had recruited some more men.

O'Brien held his gaze. "All of them," he said. "But Gabriel had went off somewhere. Looks like we let two of them out of the pasture."

"At least that's four accounted for."

O'Brien studied Sumner's handsome face. "I didn't mean to jerk any bounties out from under you. I'll sign a paper that you and me is working together. You can apply for the bounties that way."

Sumner tipped the black hat back off his forehead. "You want Luther Gabriel pretty bad, don't you?"

O'Brien thought a moment, his blue gaze seeming to pierce the glass of the whiskey bottle. "Yeah."

"I think he left the territory," Sumner said. "With Cuesta."

O'Brien nodded. "That's the way I figure it."

"He probably thinks we're in cahoots. He doesn't want to face us with Cuesta wounded."

"That makes sense," O'Brien agreed.

"But you killed his brother," Sumner continued. "And Gabriel is very family-oriented."

"Huh?" O'Brien frowned.

"It won't sit very well with him that Coot bought the ranch and you delivered the deed."

O'Brien unraveled that for a moment. "Oh.

161

Yeah, I suppose."

"He'll be back," Sumner said. "He may have an army the next time around. And he'll probably be gunning for both of us."

"I reckon," O'Brien said.

"I don't think we should give him time to regroup," Sumner said. "I think if we rode together, we'd nail his hide to a door."

O'Brien was silent.

"Gabriel will always have people with him. Helping him plot our early demise. It only makes good sense that we should put our heads together, too. And our guns."

"You just want help with them bounties," O'Brien said easily.

Sumner shook his head sidewise. "That's not all of it. Not with an animal like Gabriel. I don't know who's going to rid the territory of that bastard if it's not us. A man like that will just take over if we let him. Remember Quantrill's Raiders? We could have that right here in New Mexico."

O'Brien stared at his thick hands. "I ain't no lawman," he said. "All I know is hunting."

"That's why I need you," Sumner told him. "As for the bounties, I'm willing to put all of it on Coot, Lobo, and the other two to a purpose. It could buy that girl Annie some extra help."

O'Brien caught Sumner's sober gaze. "You'd do that?"

Sumner smiled. "Hell, it's only money."

There was a long silence between them. "I'm much obliged for that, Sumner. As a matter of fact, I'm heading out for Albuquerque next, I guess. I have to see how she's doing."

"I'd like to go with you," Sumner told him.

O'Brien looked over at the bounty hunter and realized he felt differently about him suddenly. "I wouldn't say no to that," he said. "But how would that work out with your hunt for Gabriel?"

"Just fine. It would give us time to make some plans to bring the bastard down," Sumner said. He had purposely used the plural "us" to get O'Brien's reaction to it.

O'Brien made a sound in his throat and pulled at his dark mustache. Sumner had tapered up a brown-paper cigarette and now struck a match on the tabletop. He lighted the cigarette and drew on it. He was not a heavy smoker but kept a bundle of makings for occasional use. He watched O'Brien's square face and liked the granite strength he saw in it.

"I got this friend McGraw," O'Brien began. "He says we can't kill Gabriel."

"Oh?" Sumner said, arching dark brows.

"He says Gabriel's life is charmed. Because he wouldn't kill the white buffalo."

"White buffalo?"

"There's an albino shaggy out there. Killed several men. The Indians hereabouts believe that Gabriel's safe as long as that buffalo's alive. McGraw thinks so, too."

"I'll be damned," Sumner said.

O'Brien was shaking his head. "It is kind of strange that Gabriel rode off just before I got there at Magdalena. And then found out about what happened before he come back."

163

Sumner grinned slightly. "He timed things right at Bingham, too. You don't . . . believe the white buffalo thing, do you?"

O'Brien met his quizzical look. "What I believe is that you and me is going to find that black-hearted sonofabitch and send him south," came the low, hard voice, "where he'll burn in fire and brimstone for eternity."

Sumner grinned at his new partner. "What a pleasant thought," he said.

It was already early June when O'Brien and Sumner arrived at the sanitorium in Albuquerque. The weather was warm, and Sumner had shed the outer coat that hung over his gunbelt in favor of just the vest over his blue shirt. Now the big Colt hung even more menacingly from the gunbelt. It was all over the territory that he had killed Billy Lobo, and it was generally regarded that no man could possibly go up against Certainty Sumner and live.

O'Brien did not enjoy that kind of reputation, and that sat very well with him. Few persons knew who had killed the three outlaws in Magadalena, except that it was some wild man who appeared to be more Indian than white, judging from his actions. O'Brien still kept the shotgun on his mount's irons, behind the saddle, and it would be with him now, he figured, until Luther Gabriel's corpse lay stinking up some unmarked grave.

Albuquerque was a sizeable town already. There were carriages moving up and down the main streets. Ladies in pink dresses carried parasols, and most men wore Eastern-style clothes with suit jackets and high stiff collars and ribbonlike ties at the neck. There was a buzz of business activity in the town because of banks, big stores, and stockyards.

The sanitorium was out at the edge of town to the north, and O'Brien and Sumner were received there in midafternoon on a fly-buzzing June day. The doctor in charge studied the two men with open disdain when they met him in an outer office, and he seemed reluctant to let them see Annie Seger at first.

"She is not of this world," he told them. "I'm afraid you'll be very disappointed."

"I have to see her," O'Brien insisted in his inimitable way.

The doctor asked Sumner to remove his gunbelt, and Sumner acquiesced. "I don't really have to go with you," he told O'Brien.

"No, I want you there," O'Brien said.

They all walked down a chalky white corridor to a room where a couple dozen patients were gathered. There were no men in the room, because women were segregated. They wore dull gray smocks, and many looked in bad shape. One woman went through the motions of holding and stroking an infant, but she held nothing. Another kept jerkily rising and sitting in a low rocking chair, and a third they passed suddenly lifted her smock and exposed herself to them.

There was litter on the floor everywhere, and the place had a stink to it that offended their nostrils.

In a corner they passed when leaving the room through another door, there was a bloody menstrual cloth lying in the open. The doctor made no apologies for any of it but led them on into another corridor that was not as white as the first one and had dirt and graffiti on the walls. Sumner and O'Brien exchanged sour looks.

A bulky orderly unlocked a door to a small room for them, and the doctor turned to them. "She's in here. I know you don't think much of our facility here, but remember we have a limited budget. There are better places, if you have the money to pay."

"I'd like to see her now," O'Brien said.

"She won't recognize you. She's retreated into her own world, gentlemen. There's nothing much we can do for her here."

O'Brien felt a stricture in his gut. He went on into the room, and Sumner followed. A thin female figure was seated on a chair with arms near a window. The figure did not move. O'Brien felt a tightening in his throat.

"You may have a few moments alone with her. Please don't be long. The orderly will be just outside."

O'Brien nodded, and the doctor was gone. Sumner went over to a side wall and leaned on it, and O'Brien went over and confronted Annie.

She looked like a different girl. She weighed less, and there was a dead, gaunt look about her face. Her once-lustrous and shiny hair now was stringy and dull looking. Her blue eyes stared toward the light at the window. Outside, a bird chirped in a

166

treetop, but she appeared not to hear it.

"Annie," O'Brien said.

She stared ahead.

"It's me. O'Brien."

Nothing.

"I got your letter," he said in his deep voice. "I guess you and Aaron liked the buffalo robe."

There was a flicker of understanding behind her eyes, and then she looked over at O'Brien. She focused on him, and a frown creased her thin brow.

"O'Brien?" she said in a thin, low voice.

"Yes, Annie," he said. "My friend and me come to see how you was doing."

Annie glanced past O'Brien at Sumner, then caught O'Brien's gaze again. "O'Brien," she said.

He sighed heavily. "How are you feeling, Annie?"

She did not respond. He reached out tentatively toward her to touch her arm, and she withdrew carefully. She turned away from him and resumed staring out the window.

"We brought some flowers for you," O'Brien said. "The orderly is putting them in water."

Now she had returned to that inner world in which Coot Gabriel had placed her. O'Brien glanced toward Sumner and swore under his breath. He stood there another long moment, then signaled to Sumner that they might as well leave.

Out in the corridor, O'Brien heaved his big frame against a wall for a moment and just stood there, staring at the floor. The hatred inside him for Luther Gabriel grew and threatened to burst through his chest.

"Let's go talk to the doctor," Sumner finally said.

In the outer office again, they learned that there was another hospital there in town, one with a full staff of doctors where they had had good results with people like Annie. But it cost three times what this place did, and there were no public funds available to help.

"How much would it be per month?" Sumner asked the bespectacled, elderly doctor who looked down his nose at them.

The doctor gave them a figure rather arrogantly. Sumner reached into a pouch on his belt and drew out a pile of gold coins. "How long will that keep her there?" he said.

The doctor's entire demeanor changed, and his eyebrows shot upward. He counted the money and blew out on his cheeks. "Well, there would be the cost of transfer and the paperwork and an entrance fee—"

"How long?" O'Brien said impatiently.

The doctor looked at him with a tight smile. "That should keep her there for six months."

O'Brien nodded. "All right. There will be more then, if she needs further help," he said.

"Very well, gentlemen," the doctor told them. "I'll start work on her transfer immediately.

"She'd better get over there," Sumner said in an even tone. The doctor glanced at him. "And all that money better be used to do what you said."

The old fellow nodded. "It will be, I assure you."

"What do you think her chances are over there at the private place?" O'Brien asked him.

The doctor shrugged and made a face. "A lot better than here," he said.

The two men left the hospital then and rode back downtown. They found a hitching post at one of the lesser hotels and checked in. Even that place was elegant in comparison to what either of them were accustomed, especially O'Brien, who avoided the amenities of town living as much as possible. O'Brien was particularly impressed with the interior: its sparkling chandeliers, leaded-glass windows, and polished brass.

They had a steak dinner at a nearby restaurant that evening, and O'Brien hardly spoke through it. He was feeling lower than he ever remembered feeling. They returned to the hotel after taking their mounts to a nearby livery stable and propped themselves on twin beds while Sumner read the local newspaper.

"Some woman named Jackson just wrote a book about how we've been mistreating the Indians," Sumner said, leaning against a pillow, his boots off. His Peacemaker hung on the bedpost beside his head. "It's called, *A Century of Dishonor.*"

O'Brien was renewing the edge on his boot knife with a whetstone. "I've seen a couple of dishonorable things by the red men, too," he commented absently. He did not understand Sumner's fascination with reading and trying to find out everything that was going on in the world.

"This fellow in the newspaper compares the Indians with the Russians' persecution of Jews,"

169

Sumner went on. "I find that an interesting comparison."

O'Brien gave him a narrow look. "Anybody ever tell you that you talk funny?" he said.

Sumner grinned and dropped the paper to his lap. "Sorry. I just like to remind myself once in a great while that there's something out there in the big world other than saddle leather and horse manure."

O'Brien returned the grin. "You been around in that big world a little bit, ain't you?"

Sumner sighed. "A little bit. Nobody knows this, but I lived in New Orleans for a while as a kid. I loved the place. French architecture. Creole cooking." He looked up toward the ceiling, and his aquiline face went somber. "We had to leave there."

O'Brien looked over at him.

"My Dad killed a man. A black man that worked for him. Got drunk and just killed him. For nothing. Three people saw it and got the police after him." He paused. "Jamie was my best friend, and my Dad shot him down like a dog."

O'Brien did not particularly like to hear other men's secrets. He had stopped sharpening the big knife.

"I vowed I'd never carry a gun or use one on anybody," Sumner went on. "Funny how things work out."

O'Brien put the whetstone down and ran a finger over the hunting knife, testing its edge. "My Daddy wounded a rabid dog once and was going to muzzle and gut him. I held my rifle on him and told him I'd shoot him if he killed it that way, and I meant it. He let me shoot the dog in the head. We never had any trouble like that again, and neither one of us ever told a soul about the thing. In fact, I never told no one till just this minute." He glanced over at Sumner with an odd look on his square face, as if Sumner had tricked him somehow into revealing something that was left better unsaid.

Sumner, though, felt as if the exchange had somehow brought them together closer, moved them into a more proximate alignment as men.

"I'm honored you mentioned it, O'Brien," he said.

O'Brien looked quickly away, despising himself suddenly for talking about his past. It was a thing he just never did. "I guess I finally got an edge on this," he said almost inaudibly.

Sumner smiled slightly to himself. "Where do we go from here, O'Brien?"

O'Brien put the knife down on the bed. "I'm more determined than ever after seeing Annie," he said quietly. "I won't rest easy till that godless sonofabitch fries in hell."

"I was hoping you'd say that," Sumner said. "Gabriel supposedly knows people over in Arizona Territory. I say we ride out in that direction. Maybe over toward Tombstone. I think we'll find him over that way somewhere."

O'Brien nodded. "That suits me. I'm ready to ride out tomorrow morning. I get itchy in a place like this."

"Sounds right," Sumner said. "I'll go down to the livery later and tell the hostler that—"

He was interrupted by a light knocking on their door. He and O'Brien exchanged looks. Sumner swung his legs off the bed, grabbed the Colt hanging near him, and went to the door.

"Who's there?" he said.

"It's Buffalo Bailey," came the muffled response.

Sumner looked back at O'Brien, and O'Brien nodded. "I know him," he said.

Sumner opened the door, and a grizzled fellow about his height stood there, dressed very much like O'Brien, in rawhides. He carried a Winchester slung loosely under his arm. He looked past Sumner and the Colt to O'Brien, who still reposed casually on the other bed.

"Come in," Sumner said.

Bailey came into the room, nodding his acknowledgment of the invitation. "O'Brien," he said.

O'Brien also swung his long legs to the floor. "Good to see you, Bailey." Bailey used to hunt on his own, like O'Brien and McGraw, but now worked for wages for a hide company out of Durango, up in Colorado. "What brings you into Albuquerque?"

"Oh, I just sold a load of hides for the outfit," Bailey said, scratching at his chest with his free hand. "I saw your name on the register downstairs and thought I'd bring you the news in case you didn't hear about McGraw."

O'Brien frowned slightly. "McGraw? What about McGraw?"

Bailey sighed. He looked a lot older than

O'Brien remembered him. "He's dead, O'Brien."

O'Brien rose to his feet without really knowing he had done so. "What?"

"It was that devil beast of a white buffalo," Bailey said darkly. "It killed him, O'Brien. They say he put three bullets in it, then it turned on him. It was pretty bad. It gored him up so much there wasn't hardly enough left to bury."

O'Brien just stood there numbly. "That crazy bastard," he muttered under his breath. "That bull-headed, crazy old bastard."

Chapter Nine

O'Brien took it harder than he ever would have thought about Mustang McGraw's death. He could not seem to get it out of his head for a while.

The white buffalo.

The very name was becoming anathema to O'Brien. He hated everything it stood for. It symbolized to him wild goose chases and the things greed did to men and superstitious nonsense. It was all tied in with O'Brien's pledge to get Luther Gabriel, and that was working on him in some dark, hidden place he did not even know about. That was why he had had the nightmare about it. Now, the beast had ended the life of a good and old friend. Never again would O'Brien sit with the grizzled hunter at a low-embers campfire and sip chicory coffee from a tin while they ribbed each other about missed shots or missed chances. The white buffalo had ended all that forever.

The white buffalo.

Actually, the hunter reporting the death had told O'Brien more than he wanted to know about the killing. The buffalo had almost torn McGraw's head from his shoulders. A horn had pierced McGraw's skull and shattered it, and his torso had been trampled and gored badly. O'Brien could only hope the shattered skull had come immediately, so the old hunter did not suffer a lot.

O'Brien and Sumner went ahead and left Albuquerque early the next morning, heading south and west into Arizona. But O'Brien's mind was not on what he was doing for a few days.

At the same time in Tombstone, Luther Gabriel was making plans.

He and Cuesta were holed up in a small hotel called the Longhorn, trying to keep their identities confidential. There was a lot of law in Tombstone, including Sheriff Johnny Behan and acting District Marshal Wyatt Earp. Gabriel had no fear of Behan, he was the kind of law that sided with the likes of Old Man Clanton in his rustling and other shady endeavors. Wyatt Earp, though, was another matter. The man seemed to have a passionate zeal for moral order, and Gabriel hated men like him. Earp was dangerous, too, with his brothers sworn in as deputies. Back in Dodge City, Earp had made Sumner's old friend Clay Allison back down and ride out, and he had killed a fast gunslinger named George Hoydt. Here in Tombstone, Earp had pistol-whipped a bad actor named Billy Brocius and had served notice on the

Clantons that he would not tolerate rustling in his jurisdiction, no matter how much Behan looked away.

Gabriel had heard, though, that there was some unrest among Clanton's small army of gun-slinger-cowboys, and Gabriel had come to Tombstone to recruit a few of them to take back to New Mexico and begin an outlaw empire there similar to the one Clanton was building there in Arizona. The difference being that Gabriel would not have Earp to deal with in New Mexico. He had already killed off some of the law there, and the rest of it was as weak as the U.S. paper dollar.

Gabriel would not even have come at this time, if he had not heard that Earp was gone for a while on business. Gabriel figured on coming in quietly, keeping his identity secret while he recruited a few malcontents away from Clanton, and then leaving just as quietly.

It was getting well into summer now, and it was hot and sweaty in the small hotel room that morning when Gabriel elaborated on his ideas to Cuesta. Outside on the street, heat waves already danced over the dust, and women carried parasols against the direct rays of the sun. Inside houses in town, locals fanned themselves with cardboard fans that said, "Vote for Behan," on them, and yellow dogs squeezed themselves into tight swatches of shade in cool alleys.

Cuesta, leaning against a wall on a straight chair in the still air of the hotel room, took a neckerchief and mopped his brow. He came from an area of the Sierra Madres and was not accustomed to heat. Under his shirt, he still wore a large bandage on the wound Sumner had given him, and he still felt a lot of pain whenever he moved in the wrong direction. The wound kept weeping a yellow stickiness. The doctor who had tended him first said he should have died from Sumner's bullet. But Cuesta was not the type to give up all that easily. In fact, his fond hope was that he would have a chance to kill Sumner one day, if he were just patient. He had a theory that the toughest and the most patient ended up not only as survivors, but in charge of the world.

"Did you get to talk to Purcell last night?" he said to Gabriel as he wiped at his face with the polka-dotted cloth. He had a three-days' growth of beard and looked very swarthy and blocky sitting there behind his black mustache.

Gabriel nodded. He was sitting on the edge of an unmade bed, paring his nails with a penknife. He looked particularly big and rugged sitting there with the scarred face and the dark beard and the sober, glittery eyes. He wore only a light gray shirt now in the warm weather with a small leather vest over it. Not even his brother had known it, but Gabriel had a bank account in Albuquerque where he had been salting away quite a lot of cash, which he expected to use to help finance his grand plan. Those who met him on the street, though, would have taken him for a down-and-out drifter.

"Yeah, he's meeting us at noon at the saloon. He's chewing his cud about low pay and other little complaints about Clanton, and he's got four or five others all biled up, too. He'll have them

177

with him, if he can break them all free. He's very interested in my ideas."

"Will Clanton cause us any trouble on this, *amigo?*"

Gabriel looked up at him, yawned, and scratched at his beard. "Clanton knows he's got discontents on his hands. He'll be real pleased to see them ride off, I'd guess. Purcell and another one's got Pinkertons after them, anyway. Clanton don't need no more problems than he's already got with Earp."

"I think he would like to see that badge hogtied in hell," Cuesta grinned. He thought briefly of Sumner, and the image of the bounty hunter burned into his head like hot acid for a moment. When the image was gone, so was the grin.

"I don't think we'll get crossways of Clanton," Gabriel assured him. "If we did, I reckon I could strike a deal with him. I just want to get out of here without a shootout with the Earps. My fight with the law ain't here."

Cuesta grunted. "We could be bigger than Clanton, back East. As long as we steer clear of the power in Albuquerque and Santa Fe."

"There's room for us and Albuquerque," Gabriel said.

"What about these Clanton *charros?* If they are unhappy with Clanton, will they stick with us?"

Gabriel allowed a grin to crease his own hard face for the first time. "I'm going to promise them more of everything," he said. "A real share in the operation with positions of authority. I'll tell them they'll be in on the ground floor of something real big, and they will. If they don't work out later, we'll get rid of them. If they call me on the promises, we'll get rid of them. Some will stick, and we'll use them just like Clanton did."

Cuesta returned the grin. "I like the way you talk, Luther."

Less than an hour later, the two had walked down to the nearby saloon and asked the bartender for a table back in the corner of the place, a poker table with several chairs around it. Gabriel ordered two bottles of busthead, rot-gut whiskey, and they were placed on the table with some shot glasses. Just moments later, Purcell showed up with five men.

"Glad to see you could come, Purcell," Gabriel said in his deep voice. He introduced Cuesta, and Purcell identified the men with him. Purcell himself was tall, with a narrow, bony face, and his eyebrows met over his thin nose. He carried a revolver very low on his hip because of exceptionally long arms.

Of the other five Clanton men, one was short, dumpy looking, and red-faced, and Cuesta disliked him immediately. Another one was an older man, hunchbacked and ugly, and Purcell said he had been a sergeant in the War Between the States. A third one was average looking and nondescript, with transparent eyebrows and a baby face. A fourth had a barrel chest and a boxer's nose, and wore no weapon openly. The fifth man looked like a real self-enamored gunslinger type, cocky and shifty-eyed, and wore two Navy Colt revolvers.

They all sat down after the introductions, and

Gabriel poured them whiskey all around. The young gunslinger type declined and seemed to be withholding judgment on Gabriel and Cuesta.

"You plan on setting up a system something like old N.H. Clanton's here back in New Mexico?" Purcell said, after they all had swigged at least one swallow of busthead rye.

"That's right," Gabriel told them. "There ain't hardly no law in central New Mexico. I seen to that." He grinned, and most of them returned the grin, except for the younger man. Gabriel noted it.

"We got a chance to do it even bigger there than the Clantons have here," Gabriel went on. "I don't plan to depend on rustling and stealing after we're established. I want to *run* the central counties. I'll expect my people to be sheriffs and mayors. We'll steal the way the politicians do, by taxing the hell out of the people living there. We'll bleed them, by God. And there will be swift punishment for them that don't cooperate."

"That sounds damned smart, Gabriel," Purcell said. He looked for agreement among the group and got it. Except for the young man.

"Luther here knows his business," Cuesta put in. "I've rode with him through hard times and good, *compadres*. He's got bigger ideas than any man I ever met, here or Mexico. And he knows how to make them work."

"There can be a big gap between ideas and action," the young man said arrogantly from across the table.

Gabriel and Cuesta both regarded him soberly, but neither responded to his challenge. Gabriel looked back at Purcell. "We'll gather strength as we go along. Before you know it, we'll make Clanton's operation look like penny ante. And there won't be nothing the governor can do about it, because we'll be duly elected officials of the area. We'll have the area caught in an iron fist."

"I hate to bring it up," Purcell said, "but I guess I always put money first, ever since I sucked. You figure on paying wages right at the beginning of this, Gabriel?"

Gabriel had known the issue would arise. "I got money, if that's what you're worried about," he said. "And I'll pay you twice what you got from Clanton. More later, to those of you that take on responsibility under my system. But I can't get at my capital till I get back to Albuquerque. You'll all get your pay then, and it will go back to to-day, if you join up."

Purcell thought a moment and nodded. "I reckon that would be all right with me, Gabriel," he said.

The others nodded, except for the young man. "That suits me right down to my boots," the short, dumpy fellow commented.

"It beats sitting around the Clanton ranch and reading dime novels and wondering what steers we're going to be stealing next," the barrel-chested man said in a rather high voice.

"How do we know we're going to get that double pay when we get back to New Mexico?" the young man said rather loudly.

A hush fell over the table. Purcell turned to the other man and frowned at him. "Let it go, Atkins.

I think we're all agreed we're dealing with a man of his word here."

Atkins made an offensive face. "You don't know nothing about these people," he said easily. "Except that Gabriel killed some lawmen in New Mexico. Why can't he wire for some of that capital he talks about and pay us something up front?" He looked into Gabriel's hard face and held his suddenly hostile stare.

Gabriel looked around the room. No other customers were present at the moment, and the bartender had gone out back. Gabriel scraped his chair back away from the table as the others watched silently.

"I think you're calling me a cheat and a liar," he growled.

The young fellow's face showed no fear, though. He had beaten a couple of good men in a drawdown already, and his self-confidence was almost unlimited.

"You can take it any way you want," he said, moving his own chair back and letting his hands drop to his sides. Dark, small eyes shifted about, watching Gabriel's slightest movements.

"Don't be a goddam nitwit, Atkins," Purcell said in a low voice.

But it had gone beyond reason for Atkins. In his mind's eye he could already see Gabriel going down with lead in his chest, and Atkins would be the man who killed Luther Gabriel.

"Why don't you prove what you think of me, boy?" Gabriel said.

Atkins might have passed the moment, if

Gabriel had not called him a boy. His face reddened slightly, and both hands went for leather.

In the next moment, Gabriel's hand went to his Schofield and the big gun came up pointing at Atkins's chest while Atkins was still trying to get his own iron above table level. Suddenly he wavered, his guns pointing floorward, as he stared down the barrel of the Schofield.

"Shit," he said softly, the arrogance gone in a sudden cloud of fear. He was dead, and he knew it.

In that half moment, though, the voice came to them from near the front entrance.

"What's going on back there, boys?"

Gabriel heard the voice and hesitated. His finger had been whitening over the trigger, but now he released it slightly. He glanced back of him and saw the sizeable fellow dressed in Eastern clothes with a dark hat and a gun hanging prominently on his right hip.

"Get out of here," Gabriel growled. He kept the Schofield aimed at Atkins's heart.

The newcomer ignored the command and came over to the table, his spurs rattling as he walked. "Who the hell are you people?" his voice came again.

Cuesta had gotten a better look now and nudged Gabriel from beside him. "Luther." He jerked a thumb at the newcomer's chest, where a badge was pinned.

Gabriel saw the badge and then looked into the square, beefy face. He glanced back at Atkins, and Atkins reholstered his guns. Gabriel reluctantly followed suit. He turned to the fellow standing beside him. "I might ask the same question," he said.

The square-built man with the badge narrowed his eyes down. "The name is Virgil Earp," he said easily. "Now maybe you'd like to answer my question."

Gabriel's face changed. He did not want any trouble with the Earps before he left there. He particularly did not want to square off with the brother of Wyatt Earp. "Why, we're just a couple of businessmen passing through your fair town, Marshal," Gabriel said lightly. "We met up with these cowpokes of Clanton and decided to have a drink with them. Are we doing anything illegal?"

Earp sighed slightly. "Shooting each other is a mite illegal, mister," he said. "That's what looked like was about to happen when I walked in here."

Gabriel grinned an easy grin. "Oh, no, Marshal. I was just teaching the boy here how to clear leather. Ain't that right, boy?"

Gabriel and Earp looked over at Atkins. Atkins swallowed hard and nodded almost imperceptibly. "Yeah."

Everybody else around the table kept quiet, including Cuesta.

"Well," Earp said. "There's no gunslinging allowed in Tombstone. I think you Clanton boys already know that. I'll give you an hour to leave town or turn those sidearms in."

Gabriel had heard about Wyatt Earp's rules for Tombstone but had thought he could ignore them with Wyatt gone.

"We was just going to ride on out after we had our drinks and a bite to eat," Gabriel said.

"Make sure you do," Earp said. He looked at Gabriel's face hard for a long moment, trying to remember where he had seen it before. It had been on a wanted poster, but he could not recall that on that warm summer morning. He finally turned then and left the saloon.

When he was gone, Gabriel turned back to Atkins. "You're one lucky cowboy, kid. Now get your ass out of here and don't let me ever see your peach-fuzz face again."

Atkins rose humbly and looked around the table to see if any of them would join him. Then he started past Gabriel.

"And I suggest you don't blow this around out at Clanton's place," Gabriel said as Atkins went past. "You cause me any trouble before I ride out of here, boy, and I'll find you and kill you."

The faces around the table were as somber as that of Atkins. "I'll remember that," Atkins said quietly.

Then he was gone.

When Gabriel and Cuesta and the five men rode out of Tombstone later that day heading east, Gabriel had no way of knowing that O'Brien and Sumner were riding in the opposite direction at the outer edge of the territory, directly on a collision course with him and his group.

O'Brien and Sumner had entered Arizona Territory on the previous morning. They had stopped at several small towns and stations and asked after Gabriel and Cuesta, without results. Now, on this hot summer day that seemed to burn the skin off the back of a man's neck, the two of them spotted a campfire in a clump of wild huckleberry trees where a homestead had once stood. As they rode up, they could see the remains of the log hut before they spotted the two men huddled at the fire, only twenty feet from the log ruins.

They rode on in slowly, and when the other men heard them coming, they got to their feet warily. They were rough-looking individuals, and O'Brien could see by the burros tied at the edge of the camp with equipment on their sides, that the men were prospectors. The taller of the two had a rifle in hand, and he held it at ready as O'Brien and Sumner rode up.

"Gentlemen," Sumner greeted them, tipping his dark hat back off a damp, hot forehead. His black stallion's flanks were frothy from the ride, as were those of O'Brien's Appaloosa.

The bulkier, shorter prospector without the gun nodded soberly.

"Mind if we stop and share the shade of these trees with you for a while?" Sumner went on. The man with the gun and O'Brien were eyeing each other seriously.

The prospectors looked like renegades to O'Brien, men who were unsuccessful at what they did for a living and were down on their luck. Such men, he knew from experience, often ended up robbing for profit. The two glanced at each other, and now the one with the rifle spoke.

"Why not?" he said without smiling.

O'Brien and Sumner dismounted and picketed their mounts under the nearest tree. "You wouldn't have some extra water for the animals, I guess?" Sumner said.

The shorter one started to reply, but the taller one cut in. "Nope. No extra water." He still held the rifle. Sumner wore his Peacemaker as usual, but O'Brien's weapons were on the Appaloosa, except for the knife in his boot.

"You boys can have a swig of coffee," the shorter man put in. "If you got something to drink it in." He pointed to the cooking pot of boiling chicory over the low fire.

"Much obliged," O'Brien told him.

While O'Brien went for two drinking tins from his gear, Sumner seated himself on a log beside the guttering fire. The two prospectors kept casting sidewise glances at each other, looks that were missed by Sumner as he sat down and kicked the riding kinks out of his legs.

O'Brien returned from the Appaloosa and the short prospector poured him two half-cups of chicory coffee from a boiling pot. O'Brien watched his face and did not like the looks of it. He handed one of the cups to Sumner.

"You boys picked yourselves a nice spot," Sumner said.

"We liked it," the tall man said, still holding the rifle. He had not stopped scowling since their arrival. The shorter man wore an old revolver on his hip, and his hand had settled near it since he put the pot back down.

"I see you carry digging gear," O'Brien said, sipping at the hot liquid. "Any good prospecting hereabouts?"

The tall man just stared at him without response. The shorter one shook his head. "Not around here. This ground is empty of ore as last year's bird's nest with the bottom punched out."

"You come from the west?" O'Brien said.

The short fellow nodded. "Just left Huachuca a few days ago."

The tall one frowned at him, and O'Brien noticed it.

"We're looking for a couple of men," Sumner said, also sipping at the coffee. "One of them is a fellow named Luther Gabriel. Maybe you heard his name where you came through."

The prospectors exchanged looks again, but did not respond. The taller one casually raised the muzzle of the rifle until it was aimed generally at O'Brien and Sumner. "You boys ask a lot of questions," he growled in a deep, hard voice.

O'Brien turned to him and saw the situation. The tall man now had the drop on them, and the short one now had rested his right hand on his revolver butt, and both Sumner and O'Brien had their hands full with the coffee. It appeared that the invitation to drink had been inspired by an ulterior motive.

Sumner and O'Brien exchanged a look. O'Brien sipped at the chicory again and then threw the remainder on the fire. "Sorry that bothers you," he said, "but just what the hell are you doing with

188

that gun, mister?"

Immediately after the question was asked, the short fellow drew the revolver and pointed it at O'Brien. The taller one aimed the rifle at Sumner.

Sumner rose slowly, the cup still in his hand.

"I think it's our turn to ask some questions," the short prospector sneered at them, his manner suddenly cocky.

"What is this?" Sumner said evenly. "You don't offer a man coffee and then draw down on him."

The tall, dirty-looking man came over closer. "We'll do damn well what suits us, dandy," he said.

O'Brien dropped his tin cup to the ground and faced the twosome squarely. "I figured you two for trail scum," he said.

The short fellow's face clouded over and took on a fiercer aspect than that of his companion, and he spoke harshly for the first time. "We don't take no boning from nobody, rawhide man! We're taking your mounts and your goods, and sending you and your slick partner to hell!"

Sumner discarded his cup, too. It was a bad situation, he knew. He could probably shade the short man, even with his gun out, but there was a good chance either he or O'Brien or both of them were going to get hit in the exchange of gunfire.

"You sure you want to do that, mud digger?" he said quietly.

The short man looked into Sumner's handsome face and felt an uncertainty for a moment that he could not explain. But his confidence came back quickly. "Oh, we're sure," he said.

"Well, O'Brien," Sumner said. "I reckon we'll have to find out how straight these boys can shoot."

The short man's face changed. He looked from Sumner to O'Brien, and the tall prospector was doing the same. "Did you say, O'Brien?" the short man asked.

"What's that mean to you, desert rat?" O'Brien grated out. He was preparing to rush the short fellow and let Sumner take the one with the rifle.

"Are you the buffalo hunter that killed that old boy down south of here with your bare hands?" the short man said softly.

"I don't see that that's none of your goddam business," O'Brien said ominously.

Sumner had heard that story. "That's him," he said.

The short fellow stared hard at O'Brien for a moment, then turned and glanced at his companion. He lowered his revolver and reholstered it. "We didn't know who you was, O'Brien. You can just forget what we said." He had heard an exaggerated version of the story about O'Brien killing the man down in Texas and had repeated it to the taller fellow, and they both had the idea that a man could not put O'Brien down with bullets. The tall man lowered the muzzle of the rifle.

Sumner was impressed. He smiled to himself. It was usually his reputation that stopped men cold. He figured the confrontation was over, but then he saw O'Brien walk over to the short man.

"You people got clabber for brains," he said in his deep voice. He backhanded the fellow across the face and almost broke his jaw. The short man went flying off his feet, landing hard on the ground. His eyes had widened in surprise on his way down but now squinted in raw pain.

O'Brien was not finished. He strode to the taller man, and the fellow flinched backwards. O'Brien reached and grabbed his rifle, tearing it from his grasp. With the tall man watching, he went and swung the long gun against the trunk of the nearest tree and busted it in half. He then threw the gun away from the camp. The Appaloosa whinnied nervously nearby.

Neither the tall man nor the other one said a word. They just watched O'Brien's every move with new fear. He came back to the tall fellow and stared fiercely into his face. "Now. I'll ask you the same that my partner here did. Did you hear about this Gabriel fellow where you came through?"

The tall prospector swallowed hard. He had to look up into O'Brien's cold blue eyes. "There was some mention of that name. When we was back in Bisbee."

The short fellow was sitting up on the ground nearby. He worked his jaw and was relieved it was not fractured. He had never been hit so hard in his life, and it did not escape his notice that it had been a backhand blow delivered casually.

"Gabriel was in Tombstone. We heard he was looking for men to ride with him."

Sumner came over beside O'Brien and pulled a wanted poster out of his pocket, unfolding it. He let the two men see it. "Maybe you saw him somewhere. He looks like this." On the paper was

191

a drawing of Gabriel that was quite accurate. Sumner had obtained it from his friend, Pat Garrett.

They both shook their heads. "Somebody said he would be heading back east soon into New Mexico," the short man said.

O'Brien and Sumner regarded each other thoughtfully. The short fellow regained his footing awkwardly, holding his jaw. O'Brien turned his back on them and walked over to the fire. "Okay. Now get to hell out of here."

The big man frowned, and the shorter one looked surprised. "What do you mean? This here is our camp!"

Sumner watched the exchange with pleasure. He had never ridden with anyone quite like O'Brien. O'Brien turned to the short fellow with a scowl. "Clean that dirt out of your ears, mister. I want your ugly faces out of my sight. And leave the coffee pot."

"I'll be damned!" the short fellow said.

"That don't set well in my craw," the tall man said.

O'Brien dropped a brittle look on him, and there was absolute silence for a long moment. Then, with some mutterings and low obscenities, the two picked up their gear, unpicketed their animals, and headed out.

As they rode out, O'Brien cast one last remark in their direction, while pouring himself another cup of their coffee. "Just think of this as your lucky day, boys. This fellow with me here was just about to kill you both when you finally got some sense into your heads."

The prospectors glanced at Sumner and the Peacemaker that hung across his flat belly, then they rode away without a further response.

O'Brien and Sumner knew now that they were on the right track in their hunt for Gabriel. It appeared to be just a matter of time and a little luck, and they would get their confrontation with him that they both wanted so much.

They broke camp in another hour that morning and rode out in the direction they figured would put them closer to their quarry.

In early afternoon, O'Brien got a surprise. He saw them first on the western horizon, a mass of dark bodies out there, standing on a rocky rise of ground.

"Buffalo," he said, reining up.

Sumner squinted and saw them. "They're right in our path."

O'Brien nodded.

"We'll have to ride around them, won't we?"

O'Brien was squinting his blue eyes, staring into the herd. "It's a big one, this herd," he said.

"What do you think?" Sumner asked him.

"Let's get a little closer," O'Brien said, more to himself than to Sumner.

They rode on, and the herd grew bigger. The wind was coming from the herd, so O'Brien knew they could get quite close without alarming the shaggies. He was searching the herd with his gaze now, and suddenly he stopped again.

"Sonofabitch," he muttered. "It's there."

Sumner looked over at him, sitting tall on the Appaloosa. "What's there?"

"The white buffalo," O'Brien said grimly. "Look. Over there to the south."

Sumner looked, and he saw it. It looked twice as big as the next biggest animal, and its snow-white coat shone in the summer sun. "I'll be damned," he whispered. He turned to O'Brien. "That's it? That's the animal that killed your partner?"

"That's it," O'Brien said. "I heard it was seen over this way."

"It's the damnedest thing I ever saw," Sumner said.

"It happens once in a while in nature," O'Brien said. "Some find the color pleasing to the eye."

"But you don't?" Sumner said.

O'Brien was somber. "I knew a man once. Had white hair and pink eyes and they called him Rabbit. He was one of the most senseless killers I ever heard of. Just like this shaggy."

Sumner regarded him seriously. "Why don't we just ride around them? We've got other things to think about."

O'Brien grunted. "I want to get just a little closer."

He rode off toward the herd slowly, and Sumner reluctantly followed. O'Brien got within two hundred yards, stopped, and dismounted. He stared ahead, and now the white buffalo was right on the near edge of the herd and looking right at him.

Sumner rode up and dismounted, too. O'Brien

pulled the big Sharps carbine from its saddle scabbard, and it looked like an elephant gun to Sumner.

"Do you want to get involved in this?" Sumner said from behind O'Brien.

O'Brien was now drawing a slim tripod from the same double scabbard and placing it on the ground. "This hell beast killed McGraw," he said. "It would pleasure me quite a lot to take it down." He affixed the big heavy gun to the tripod, working fast now. He got down on one knee and sighted along its long barrels. The gun weighed sixteen pounds and was custom-made just for O'Brien. It fired with accuracy at five hundred yards.

"Well," Sumner said, "the bounty on its hide does beat some on men I chase down."

"The animal is a killer," O'Brien said simply. "A danger to every hunter that goes after it. It wouldn't be right to have him in my sights and just pass him by." He slipped two big cartridges into the breech of the gun and slammed them home.

"Hey, he's separated himself from the herd," Sumner said. "He sees you, O'Brien. He's moved this way."

"I know," O'Brien said. He sighted along the barrels and eased his finger onto the triggers.

"I'll get your Winchester and back you up," Sumner said.

"The hell you will," O'Brien said, turning to him. "You can shoot fast and straight, Sumner, but that's just a little part of this. Get on that stallion and fall back fifty yards or so. Give me some elbow room."

Sumner held O'Brien's sober gaze and realized he could not talk to him. O'Brien was being guided by his underjaw and the back of his stiff neck right now.

"Right," Sumner finally replied. He remounted the black stallion and moved off behind O'Brien for a small distance, and the Appaloosa followed him.

The herd was acting a little skittery now, and the albino had moved directly at O'Brien, getting a better look at him. It came to within a hundred-fifty yards and then closer yet. O'Brien sighted down the barrels of the long gun, and the buffalo pawed the ground and snorted.

O'Brien got the big animal in his sights and was awed by its size and hostile appearance. The reports on it were not exaggerated. It was a monster, a white monster with enormous, curving horns and a hump that looked like a mountain. It definitely had spotted him.

O'Brien zeroed in on the big white chest and saw the red eyes flashing pure hatred toward him. He carefully squeezed the trigger.

There was a loud explosion, and the white buffalo jumped and then fell onto its side. The herd reacted wildly and began running in all directions but not at O'Brien. O'Brien started to rise off his knee, and then he saw the albino struggle to its feet. He frowned, unbelieving. The buffalo made a loud snorting and grunting sound, a wild, primordial sound, and then it was coming

196

right at him, charging, great head lowered.

O'Brien got behind the gun again, found the charging buffalo in his sights, and squeezed the other trigger. The hammer fell on a dud cartridge, and the gun misfired. O'Brien swore aloud, and then the buffalo was on him.

It looked like Mount Whitney when it arrived. The big head was down low, ready to impale him on its sweeping horns, the red eyes maniacal. O'Brien rolled to his right at the last possible moment, and then the gun and tripod went flying, the hooves thundering all around him, it seemed. The left horn ripped into his rawhides and tore at the flesh of his arm. It was like being clubbed with a broadsword. Then the animal had swept past with dust flying all about O'Brien. It pounded past for about ten yards, then turned to finish him off.

O'Brien realized he was in trouble in that moment. He struggled to his knee. Just as the buffalo began its second charge, he saw the black stallion coming, from the corner of his eye.

Sumner was on the horse, reaching down for O'Brien. "O'Brien! Come aboard! Now!"

In the next instant, O'Brien grabbed out at Sumner's arm and fastened an iron grip on it. Then he was swinging onto the mount's rump behind Sumner. Just as he got seated, the stallion's eyes wild, dust flying, the big white buffalo arrived. The stallion was galloping now, but the two animals met at a juncture near the overturned Sharps and tripod, and one horn sliced along the horse's flank as it sped past. The stallion almost

197

went over with the weight of the two men on it, but it regained its footing, still on the run, and galloped off.

The buffalo wheeled again, and as Sumner reined up fifty yards away, both men watched as the buffalo attacked the gun and tripod, punching the gear into the air and then trampling on it. Finally, seeing that the men were not available to charge any longer, it turned and ran off to join the herd, which was disappearing over a small hill to the north.

O'Brien slumped on the rear of the stallion and shook his shaggy head, which was bareheaded now. His rawhides were badly torn on the right side, and blood ran down his right arm and into the palm of his hand. He was dust covered and looked like he had been run over by a wagon. "Goddam," he grunted out.

Sumner watched the buffalo disappear from sight. "My God," he said quietly. "If Luther Gabriel's life is charmed as long as that animal roams the plains, he might live to be a very old man."

Chapter Ten

Later that evening, in hardship camp out on the trail, O'Brien finally worked a bandage of sorts onto the arm wound with Sumner's help. They had gathered water at a shallow stream, and now were able to wash some dust off in a multipurpose pan. O'Brien had warmed his insides with some flask whiskey and was feeling good. This was his kind of day. They made a fire, ate beans from a tin, and put some hardtack down. O'Brien boiled some real coffee, which was the only part of the meal Sumner enjoyed. Unlike O'Brien, he had never taken to nights on the trail. He appreciated a bed under his back and decent food. O'Brien was in his element and generally despised the oases of civilization that Sumner preferred to the trail.

"I guess that evens the score up," he commented to Sumner after they had eaten and were both propped against a granite boulder near the fire, watching the flames flicker down and sipping at their coffee cups.

Sumner glanced toward him quizzically. They were both bareheaded now. Sumner's hair was slicked back and looked even darker than usual. O'Brien's was uncombed and rather wild looking, as always.

"You saved my life out there. That white devil was about to grind me into the dust, tear me up like he did McGraw."

"He did seem to have things under control," Sumner grinned. "I've never seen anything like that. That animal must be half grizzly."

"I'm glad you was there," O'Brien told him, looking seriously into Sumner's dark eyes.

"Hell, you'd have done the same for me. Matter of fact, you did," he grinned. He was looking at a newspaper he had picked up in the last town they had passed through.

O'Brien grunted. He felt close to Sumner now, had accepted him as completely as he had McGraw. "I guess both of us have been kind of lucky that way." He did not understand exactly why he liked Sumner. They were very different kinds of men, he knew, and O'Brien had never befriended a man who looked and talked like Sumner. He had particularly steered clear of gunslingers, which Sumner was.

"I never got caught like that before," O'Brien went on.

Sumner glanced over at him. A man felt safer out on the trail just being with O'Brien. "I never realized there was so much—risk in buffalo hunting."

O'Brien smiled tiredly. "There can be times out

there." He looked into the fire, and the flames reminded him of a very tense time for him out on the hunt. He began remembering it out loud.

"A prairie fire almost got me once. I didn't know it was coming, I was so busy with the hunt. I took down three animals in a small herd and was about to do some skinning. Then the scent come to me."

Sumner looked over and O'Brien was staring into the fire. "By the time I realized I was in trouble, it was bright out there on the horizon, that ring of flame. Smoke climbing to the sky. I was cut off from my mount, and I knew I couldn't outrun it. There was a wind, and it was coming too fast."

Sumner had become interested. "What did you do?"

"The only thing I could think of. I turned to the shaggy I was kneeling beside, slit the belly wide open, and gutted it. By that time, the fire was on me. I crawled into that dead beast's insides and let the skin come closed. Then the fire was there.

"It was like a roaring Hades for about five minutes. That animal's insides heated up like an oven, and the smoke almost got me. When I come out, my rawhides was singed almost black, and my arms and face looked like I just been out in the desert." He looked over at Sumner and grinned. "That shaggy was cooked to perfection, all the skin burned off. And the prairie was black all around me. It took me four days to find my horse."

Sumner regarded O'Brien with renewed respect. "I guess you had some luck that day."

O'Brien shrugged. "I reckon. There's a hundred ways to give it over out there, and not many of them is pretty." He looked at Sumner. "But there must be some tight times in your line, too."

Sumner grunted. "It can get tricky some days." He was looking through his newspaper as he spoke now. "I thought my owl-hoot days were over when Curly Quentin's brother finally caught up with me."

O'Brien regarded him soberly. "So you're the man that killed Curly Quentin."

Sumner turned a page and nodded. "His brother swore revenge, and one day I walked into a place and had three guns surrounding me. Quentin and two drifters were going to sieve my insides up good." He shook his head. "I still don't know how I walked away from that. I took a bullet, and a second one nicked me. But when I left that place, the three of them had saddled their last mount."

O'Brien smiled slightly. Sumner would do to ride the trail with, he decided.

Sumner had already forgotten the story. His handsome face looked surprised. "Well, I'll be damned. Remember my old friend Pat Garrett? You met him at Duran."

O'Brien nodded. "I remember."

"Well, that bastard finally did it. He killed Billy the Kid."

O'Brien looked from Sumner down to the paper, regarding its mysteries balefully.

"He caught the Kid at Fort Sumner. He had had him in custody two or three times before, and the Kid escaped by killing. Santa Fe and Lincoln, he slipped away from. Murdered two guards at Lincoln. But Pat found him at Pete Maxwell's place and shot him dead in his own bedroom. They're saying Pat didn't give him a fair chance to surrender and that Billy was unarmed."

O'Brien regarded Sumner with a surprised look. "There ain't no shame in that. Your friend Garrett had a responsibility. He wasn't in no shooting contest. He got fed up with Billy, that's all."

Sumner caught O'Brien's steady look and nodded. He liked the analysis. "I agree. But the papers are pestering Pat about it. It shows how much appreciation there is out there for getting a dirty job done." He put the paper down. "You can expect the same kind of thing if we don't bring Luther Gabriel in alive."

O'Brien's face clouded over some with repressed frustration and anger. "I ain't making no arrests if we find that sonofabitch," he said flatly. "I want that clear right now, Sumner."

Sumner nodded. "I know. You can rest easy on that score. When we meet, it will be them or us."

O'Brien slid down so that he was lying with just his head propped against the boulder, his neck resting on a rolled blanket. He closed his blue eyes against the light of the guttering fire. "If we don't send that bastard to hell," he said under his breath, "there ain't no use in having one."

It was not much later, farther west in Arizona, that Luther Gabriel was making plans to ride back into New Mexico. The heat of late summer was boiling across the land now, though, and Gabriel was hoping for a break in the weather before he rode east.

He had been unsuccessful in the recruitment of any more men after hiring on the Clanton riders and had decided to wait until he was back in more familiar territory now before attempting to enlarge his gang. At this point it was just him, Cuesta, the Clanton man Purcell, and the four men he had brought with him from the Clanton ranch.

The gang was presently holed up in a miner's abandoned shack not far east of Douglas in southern Arizona. Gabriel had been planning a small holdup of an express station nearby for the next day to get some finances for the trip east when he got the news about O'Brien and Sumner. He was in the shack alone with Cuesta when Purcell rode up outside and came in.

Cuesta had drawn his Mauser revolver, then replaced it as he recognized Purcell's narrow, bony face.

"I just come out to give you some news," Purcell told them as he threw himself onto a rickety straight chair at the table where they sat drinking. Hard sunlight fell on the rough-hewn floor in bright bars.

"Yeah?" Gabriel said, uninterested.

"There's two men asking after you, Gabriel," Purcell said.

Gabriel looked up and met Purcell's serious gaze. He carefully placed his shot glass down before him. "What two men?" he said quietly.

"One of them's a gunfighter," Purcell said.

"Name of Sumner. And he's got a buffalo hunter with him."

Gabriel's face had gone dark. He and Cuesta exchanged black looks. "Jesus Christ!" Cuesta breathed out fearfully.

Gabriel looked back at Purcell quickly. "Where were they seen?" he asked.

"In a little town due east of here. Word is, they were heading out in this direction today."

Gabriel mulled that for a moment. "That would bring them here tomorrow sometime," he said to himself. "Hell, that's when we'll be in Douglas, hitting that express station."

"Well, at least there's seven of us," Cuesta said in his accented English. "Let them come on into Douglas. Maybe we'll be finished at the station."

"Yeah, and maybe not," Gabriel said. He thought for a moment. "If I remember right, there's a low, rocky pass just east of here about ten miles. Sumner and O'Brien will be riding through that narrow gap on their way here."

"So what?" Cuesta said.

"So some of us will be out at that pass, and the rest will take that express station," Gabriel said, "and then we won't have to be looking over our shoulders all the time. That goddam hunter ain't going to rest easy till he's done something about that agent we killed in Stinking Creek. I heard they went all the way back to Tennessee together, and them billies stick as close as horse glue to one another."

"And that other one just wants the bounties on us," Cuesta said bitterly. "That is the lowest kind of snake on the prairie, *amigo*, that will hunt a man for money."

"Well, after tomorrow, his goddam bounty collecting will be finished," Gabriel muttered. "I just wish I could be there, damn it. But I can't trust nobody else at that station, not even you, Cuesta."

"You're going to split us tomorrow?" Cuesta said. "You can't carry water on both shoulders, *compadre*. We have to do one thing or the other, *verdad?*"

Gabriel shook his square head. "It won't take but three of us to take that station. I'll take you and one of the Clanton boys, maybe the sergeant." He looked up at Purcell. "You and the other three will go meet our hunters at the rock pass. I want you to get there early and split up on either side of the trail where it passes through the outcroppings. Let them both get up where you can't miss them. Then shoot to kill. Don't let them see you before it all starts. They should be easy to take down as long as you surprise them."

Purcell nodded his head. "Sounds right to me."

"Go get the others and we'll tell them," Gabriel said.

O'Brien and Sumner, knowing nothing of the ambush, slept well that night on the trail. Early the next morning, on a sweltering late summer day, they headed toward Douglas, where they hoped to get some hard information about Gabriel.

They had been riding for almost two hours that

morning, through a blast-furnace heat, when they arrived at the pass where there were large boulders on either side of the trail. When O'Brien saw the rocks, he stopped the Appaloosa and tipped his trail-colored Stetson back on his shaggy head for a moment and mopped his brow. Sweat ran down the sides of his face and down his body under his clothing. He did not notice much, he was used to it. Sumner, stopping beside him, was slumping in the saddle, not paying a lot of attention to the trail. O'Brien glanced at the rocks, squinting in the glare of sun. He was always careful when he passed cover on the trail. He saw nothing.

He turned to Sumner. Sumner's face was flushed with the heat, and he looked very uncomfortable.

"We could rest here, find some shade in them rocks," O'Brien told him. "But we're not that far from Douglas. Would you care to ride on in?"

Sumner nodded, resettling his dark hat on his wet hair. "Let's get it over with, partner." He turned a handsome smile on O'Brien. "I'm looking forward to a cold ale in town."

O'Brien returned the smile. "Let's ride, then," he said.

Sumner spurred the black stallion and headed on up a slight grade between the rocks. O'Brien caught him partway there, and they rode into the low pass together, side by side.

When they got halfway through, with the rocks on either side of them as close as twenty to thirty yards, O'Brien scanned the outcroppings again, then reined in suddenly. He had seen just a brief flash of metal in the hard sun, up in the rocks to their right.

"Hold it!" he yelled at Sumner.

Sumner was just five feet ahead of O'Brien. In the next instant, there was a gunshot from the rocks on their left, and hot lead hit Sumner in the left chest, ruptured his aorta, and traveled downward through his torso, tearing and ripping through him like a hot branding iron. He was jerked sidewise when hit, and then his mount was rearing, and Sumner was falling to the hard ground.

O'Brien just had time to register all of that in his head and reach for the Winchester on the Appaloosa's irons when the next shot rang out. The shot nicked his right shoulder and made the Appaloosa plunge, then the second shot came and hit him like a baseball bat in the right side.

He was knocked off the Appaloosa with that hit, and was thrown to the dust within a few feet of Sumner. The Appaloosa was running off now, and the black stallion had shied away toward the nearby rocks. Another shot came and hit Sumner, and O'Brien could see his body jump in the dirt. Then O'Brien felt a blackness welling over him, and he lost consciousness.

The four riders came out of the rocks then, standing their mounts over the inert forms of Sumner and O'Brien. It was Purcell, the short red-faced man, the fellow with the baby face, and Skinner, the barrel-chested fellow with the boxer's nose. They all carried rifles.

The baby-faced one grinned over at Purcell.

"That was like shooting ducks in a pond."

Purcell nodded. "You and Skinner make sure. Gabriel would want us to."

The two to whom he had given instructions dismounted, taking the rifles with them. Skinner went and stood over O'Brien, and Baby Face went up to Sumner. A low moan issued from the depths of Sumner's chest.

"This one might be alive," Baby Face said. He aimed the rifle at Sumner's dark hair, and squeezed off a round. The body jumped again, and the back side of Sumner's skull was blown away. The other ugly man aimed his rifle at O'Brien's chest and fired, hitting the buffalo hunter squarely. O'Brien's left hand twitched for a moment, as if clawing at the dirt, and then the hunter was still.

"That ought to do it," Purcell said evenly. "Come on, let's ride on back and tell Gabriel the good news."

It was just moments later that they rode off, thundering through the low pass on their way back to the rickety shack outside of Douglas.

Chapter Eleven

Luther Gabriel had had some good luck, too, in Douglas. While his underlings were about their business of ambushing O'Brien and Sumner, Gabriel was busy robbing the express station. The agent had unexpectedly left for the morning, so there was no killing and no identification of the gang. Gabriel found a sizeable cash box there, shot it open, and recovered several hundred dollars in gold and silver.

When Purcell reported that his group had killed O'Brien and Sumner out on that hot trail, Gabriel could not believe his luck. He had wanted O'Brien badly, and Sumner, too, but he had also known that they were dangerous to him. Now the danger was past, and the biggest obstacle to his returning to New Mexico and taking over a large part of the territory had been overcome. Now he would return there triumphant in many ways, and it would not be long until he was the most powerful force in the whole area.

He was so sure of himself now that he took his men into Douglas that evening and bought them all the drinks they could put down. The robbery at the express station had been discovered, but the local sheriff and his single deputy had not shown themselves to Gabriel about it yet.

The saloon where they drank that night was loud and noisy, because it was Saturday night and a lot of cowboys were in from nearby ranches. There was a piano player against one wall and a couple of rather plain hostesses who did not appeal to Gabriel or Cuesta; some customers were busy losing their money at a faro table at the rear of the place. The saloon was one of those places with sawdust on a plank floor, and hand-rived rafters overhead. Gabriel and his men sat at two adjacent tables and drank cheap whiskey. Gabriel was feeling very good.

"I'm telling you, Cuesta," he was saying loudly to his right-hand man that evening, "everything is finally going right. I can feel it in my gut. Nothing can stop us now."

Cuesta swigged some whiskey directly from a bottle. His swarthy face was bright with a wide grin. "Maybe that Indian was right," he said. "About you and that buffalo. I just read it's gone up in the mountains where nobody will ever find it, *amigo*. You're living under its charm, and it looks as if it will go on forever. *Siempre*, my friend."

"Maybe you're right," Gabriel agreed. "Because tonight, by Jesus, I feel immortal!"

At the next table, the grizzled ex-sergeant let out

a loud whooping call and pulled a hostess onto his lap. At the table with Gabriel were only Cuesta and Purcell. Purcell grinned at the ex-sergeant and held a whiskey glass up toward Gabriel.

"Here's to your future, Luther," Purcell said. "And ours."

"I'll drink to that," Gabriel said through his dark beard. He clacked his glass against Purcell's, and so did Cuesta. They all swigged the drinks down.

Gabriel stared at the empty glass. "I see us breaking off that southern part of the territory and making it a goddam separate government," he said quietly. "We'll gather men around us and enforce our own martial law. You boys will be my enforcers. Why should the government at Santa Fe get all the taxes from them fat ranchers? They can, by God, share it all with us."

Purcell grinned. "We'll make our own goddam rules."

The hostess at the next table yelled loudly, rose from the ex-sergeant, and slapped his face hard. He and the others laughed loudly as she hurried off to the bar. The piano was playing a lively ditty from the Civil War, and the whole place was merry.

"There are fine times ahead, *cierto*," Cuesta said boisterously. "We will—"

He paused, looking past Gabriel toward the front doors. "I think the sheriff has at last ventured from his hiding place," he said, lowering his voice.

Gabriel looked and saw the middle-aged sheriff

at the swinging doors, a star on his vest. Beside him stood a young skinny fellow who was his deputy. They both wore guns, and the deputy was carrying a Henry .44 Rifle under his arm.

"Uh-oh," Purcell said. Suddenly the noise at their next table dissipated into silence as Gabriel's men also saw the lawmen. In fact, the general racket throughout the place seemed to quiet in that moment. The sheriff looked toward Gabriel's tables and then walked directly toward them, the deputy right behind him.

"Evening, boys," the older fellow said when he reached the table. He was not impressive looking. His hips were wide, and he had a belly. He wore a dark mustache on his lip that was very short, giving him a rather comical appearance.

"Sheriff," Gabriel said.

"I guess you boys are new hereabouts," the sheriff said.

"Yeah, that's right, we're just kind of passing through," Gabriel said roughly.

"Are you the ones that's sleeping out at the old St. Clair mine?" the sheriff went on. His deputy came up beside him, looking a little wary of Gabriel and his people.

"Yeah, you're right again," Gabriel said openly. "We come from Tombstone, and we're on our way into New Mexico to get jobs on a ranch there. We already got an offer. But we wanted to rest our mounts for a few days here. There ain't no law against us using that shack, I guess?"

The sheriff shook his head. "No, there ain't." He studied Gabriel's face. "I'm here to ask if you know anything about that robbery out at the express station earlier today."

Gabriel furrowed his thick brow. "Robbery? Hell, Sheriff, we don't even know where the express station is. That right, boys?"

"That is correct, Sheriff," Cuesta put in.

"We don't know nothing about *nothing!*" the short red-faced gang member said from the next table, wearing a big grin.

The sheriff frowned toward the other table. He did not like the looks of this group. He turned his sober look back onto Gabriel. "Maybe a couple of you better come on down to the office with me," he said slowly. "Just for some questioning. It's just routine, you understand."

Gabriel's face took on a hard look. "No, I can't say I do understand, Sheriff. Is it your purpose to just come and bother any man that you don't know by sight, just because somebody robbed your express office? I just don't give that credence."

The deputy looked worried. The sheriff licked a dry mouth. Gabriel was the kind of man that people would cross the room just to avoid, if they saw him coming. "This ain't no harassment, boys. Just you come along, mister," he said, indicating Gabriel, "and your partner here." He gestured toward Purcell.

Gabriel shook his head sidewise. "Mister, if you was out on the street without that badge, you couldn't flag down a gut wagon," he said slowly. "Now why don't you just let it go?"

The deputy looked quickly to the sheriff to see

his reaction. There was renewed fear in his thin face.

"You boys are feeling a little juicy, I see," the sheriff stalled. "But that saucy manner won't get you far in this town."

Gabriel laughed a very hard laugh. "Sheriff, you'll have to excuse us, we got drinking to do."

Most of the noise had subsided around them now, and other customers had become interested in the exchange. The sheriff glanced at his deputy and stood there awkwardly. "Well, let me ask you right here, then," he finally said. "Did you boys have anything to do with that robbery at the express station?" He was trying to save face, and everybody knew it.

Gabriel put an innocent look on his bearded face. "Why, hell, no, Sheriff. We're just a bunch of cowpokes out of work and looking for some peace and quiet here before moving on."

"That is right, Sheriff," Cuesta put in. "Why, we are so *simpaticos* we would not swat a fly in your nice town."

All the Clanton men laughed at that and some of the other customers, too.

The sheriff's aging face colored slightly, but he backed away from a confrontation. "Well. If we get any hard evidence about this, we may want to talk again."

But Gabriel would not let him off the hook entirely. "Don't come and bother me with this no more, Sheriff," he said in a growl.

Another long, uncomfortable pause. Then, "I'll

just see how it goes, boys." Then the sheriff was striding back out of the place to the derisive laughter of the gang and many others present.

The very next morning early, at a time when Gabriel was still sleeping off his liquor outside of Douglas, two trail drifters heading for Tombstone approached the low pass with the boulders on either side, out east of Douglas, and reined up short when they saw the two still figures on the ground. They stared warily at the inert forms of O'Brien and Sumner.

"What we got here?" the huskiest one of them said, squinting down on the dark objects.

There were three vultures circling high up against the cobalt sky. They wheeled and pirouetted up there in spiral circles, assessing the scene below with hungry, greedy eyes.

"Looks like a couple of corpses," the thinner drifter said. He looked around, scanning the rocks. "Let's go take a look-see."

They rode on up to the deathly forms. The figure of O'Brien lay with one leg up under it, the eyes closed, and the sand around it was stained darkly with blood. Sumner's body lay in a second dark, sticky pool, and there were blowflies humming about it, laying eggs in the skull.

"They're dead, all right," the husky man said. "I never seen none no deader."

"Looks like they was ambushed," the other fellow commented. He looked again up at the rocks.

"This one over here wears a Peacemaker," the husky one said. "No need letting that set there, he won't be needing it." He dismounted and went and unbuckled the gun and holster from Sumner's dead body, making a face at the mess he saw and brushing at flies that hummed around his head. His companion dismounted, and stood over O'Brien.

"These stovepipe boots is just what I been looking for, myself," he grinned. "And there's a bowie in one of them." He reached down and pulled and jerked on the boots, making the still form of O'Brien jump about. Finally he had them off and was pulling them onto his own feet after removing a pair of low, worn ones. The husky man had strapped the Peacemaker onto his waist.

"There, by Jesus," he said. "You never know what good luck lays in store. Now let's ride out of here before somebody comes along and thinks we done this."

The other man nodded, and they remounted. The boots were a little big for him, but they were the best pair he had ever owned. "Let's get into Douglas," he said. "I got an awful thirst."

Soon the dark figures on the ground were alone again. Within a half-hour one of the vultures had landed beside Sumner's body and began pecking at the ashen-hued but still handsome face. A second bird alighted beside O'Brien and waddled over to the hunter's form, jabbing a couple of times at O'Brien's side.

But it was just moments later that the Conestoga hove into view and rumbled on up the grade

217

toward the bodies. The wagon had come from the same direction as the drifters and was heading west. The wagon was hauled by a four-horse team, and a young man and his wife were seated on the buckboard. They came almost up to the two grisly forms before they stopped.

"Holy Jesus!" the young man whispered. "Don't look, Addie!"

His bride of six weeks turned pale but did not avert her face from the sight. "If you want me to live out here in the territory with you, Jared, you can't hide the world from me."

They were headed to a land grant west of Tombstone, and the young man wanted to farm for his living. The couple had come from Kansas City and were just learning what the wild country was like.

He got off the wagon and went and stood over the dark forms. "Something awful happened here, Addie," he said over his shoulder. He looked up and saw the vultures up there, circling and staring with ugly little eyes.

"We can report it to the authorities in Douglas," she said from the buckboard.

He shook his head. "By that time, there won't be nothing left of them," he said. "No, the only Christian thing to do is bury them, Addie. I'll just get my pick and shovel from the wagon."

She sighed heavily. She wore a gingham dress and a light-hued bonnet to protect her pretty face from the sun. "I'll help," she said quietly.

The young man called Jared dragged the two bloody forms over behind the nearest rocks to a sandy place where he could dig. He dug a double-wide grave, sweating under the climbing sun. It was hard work, but he felt it was something he would want someone to do for him. Addie kept the flies off the two figures and handed Jared the pick when he needed it. Finally he had a double grave dug. He dragged Sumner's body into it, and it puffed up dust when it hit bottom there. Jared stared at the once-handsome face and shook his head, then turned to go over to O'Brien's still form. "You can say some words over them, Addie, after I get them covered," he was saying.

But when he glanced at his wife, she was staring down at O'Brien's figure in shock.

"What is it?" he said. He grabbed O'Brien's stockinged leg to drag him into the grave.

"Its . . . hand moved," Addie said in fear.

He looked down at O'Brien and smiled slightly. "Its nerves. They do that to corpses. When I was a kid, I saw a corpse move its arm. It was all muscles and nerves jerking around after death. The undertaker tried to explain it to me." He started dragging O'Brien into the grave. Halfway there, the low, almost inaudible sound issued from O'Brien's chest.

Jared jumped back, releasing his hold on O'Brien's leg. Addie gave a little yell. "There! You heard it too, didn't you?"

"Jesus!" Jared whispered. He rubbed a hand across his mouth.

"I'm telling you, he's alive!" Addie said almost hysterically.

"He can't be!" Jared said. "He's got two holes in

him, and either one could have killed him!"

Addie went and bent over O'Brien's grayish face, opening his mouth with her fragile hand. She leaned down with her ear next to his mouth, and then the sound came again, a little louder. She jumped away again. "There, again!" she breathed.

Her young husband stared in awe. "You're right. He ain't give it up yet. We can't bury him."

"Well, of course not!" she said.

He looked over at her. "Addie, there's no way he's going to make it shot up like this. It's just a matter of time."

"Well, I'm not going to sit out here in the sun hoping he's going to die so I won't get sunstroke!" she said excitedly. "Let's take him in to the nearest town and let them have him. If he dies on the way, they can bury him."

Jared hesitated. "Well, I guess you're right. But you'll have to help me get him aboard the wagon."

They struggled to get O'Brien's massive form aboard the Conestoga and finally had him bedded down aboard. Jared then buried Sumner's corpse so the big birds could not get at it, and they were about to leave when they heard the whinny from behind the rocks. Jared went and found the Appaloosa standing there, nervous and uncertain. He brought it over to the wagon, found the Sharps carbine on the irons, and realized the horse probably belonged to the hunter they had just put aboard the wagon. Jared tethered the Appaloosa to the back of the Conestoga, and then they headed off on a detour to the north to a village that was about half the distance of Douglas. Addie thought that would give O'Brien a better chance to make it.

On the way, Addie stuffed cloth into O'Brien's wounds, because he was still slowly bleeding. Whereas Sumner had been dying from the moment the first shot ruptured his aorta, the head shot finishing him off in a moment, O'Brien had been more fortunate. The shot in his side had missed all vital organs by just fractions of inches and exited six inches farther back, busting a posterior rib. The one the barrel-chested gunman had fired into his chest had missed his heart by another inch, fractured an anterior rib, and collapsed his left lung.

As Jared had conjectured, either of those hits would probably have killed an ordinary man. But O'Brien was far from ordinary. In his coma, from some dark place where he had never been, he was fighting for his life. And he would not give up.

O'Brien had a third wound, a shallow one in the shoulder that chipped bone and took away a small amount of flesh, but that did not figure in his fight for his life.

The Conestoga arrived in the tiny town of Spaulding a couple of hours after the still O'Brien was loaded aboard it, and O'Brien had another bit of luck without even knowing it. There was a local citizen there named Foley who had once worked in a hospital in the east as a nurse. It had been years since the rather elderly, gray-grizzled fellow had tended any sick or wounded, but when Jared and Addie presented their case to him and showed him the limp form of O'Brien, Foley agreed to take

O'Brien into his cabin and tend him. Jared offered him a few silver dollars, and Foley refused them.

"As long as I've got food, he can share it," Foley told them. "The main thing is to get them wounds closed."

The young couples went on west that evening, leaving O'Brien in Foley's care. Foley dug the slug out of O'Brien's chest and sewed up O'Brien's wounds, putting poultices on the drain openings. He figured O'Brien would be dead in twenty-four hours. Tough men often hung on for days after a bad shooting, only to give it up in the end.

But O'Brien did not give it up. Deep in his coma, he fought back. He fought the fever that racked him that night and for several nights to come, and he willed his body to heal his deep wounds. The collapsed lung began healing the hole in it. Within five days, it began taking in air again and holding it.

After two days, Foley began hearing moaning sounds from O'Brien's chest, then his lips began trying to form words. Foley, sitting on a chair beside the bed in which O'Brien lay, his bed, would shake his head and wish O'Brien would give it up. When he had told Jared he would share his provisions with O'Brien, he had not really thought it would ever come to that. But then one morning O'Brien's eyelids fluttered, and he opened his blue eyes for a moment and looked right at Foley. Then he passed out again. That same evening, Foley spoon-fed him some soup, and O'Brien managed to get some of it down.

From that moment onward, it was clear that

O'Brien was going to make it. The next day, O'Brien opened his eyes again and looked around him.

"Where . . . am I?" he said in a half-croaking whisper.

"It don't matter where you are," Foley told him. "You're in good hands. Just keep resting. You're going to recover, by God."

O'Brien began remembering. He saw Foley come, sit down beside the bed on a straight chair, and stare down at him. "You been through hell, mister."

O'Brien regarded the old fellow soberly. Foley was bent and crippled looking. He had many lines in his weathered, gray-bearded face. He wore sloppy farm clothing, but it all looked clean.

"They . . . ambushed us," O'Brien said, thinking it through. "It must have been . . . Gabriel's men."

"You're lucky to be alive," Foley told him. "If that young couple didn't bring you in, you'd be buzzard feed by now."

"Sumner," O'Brien said. "What about Sumner?"

"I guess that would be the one they found with you. He wasn't so lucky. He's dead and buried out there."

O'Brien made a face and closed his eyes against the awful truth of Sumner's death. "Sonofabitch," he muttered.

"I got your Appaloosa out back in a shed," Foley said, "and the gear that was on it."

O'Brien nodded. He could not believe it. Men

were hard to find you could ride with and not worry about their being trustworthy. Sumner was one of them. He had become a friend to O'Brien, and O'Brien realized, lying there, that he had suffered a great loss.

"The name is Foley," Foley said. "You can stay here till you're able to ride."

O'Brien focused on him. "Call me O'Brien," he said. "And I'm much obliged for the help, Foley."

Foley shrugged. "You been a kind of challenge to me. I liked it."

It was only a week later, much to Foley's surprise, that O'Brien got up out of the bed and began trying to get about. His wounds were still draining, and he was very weak. His square face was pale, and he went about with big, thick bandages on his torso and side. But day by day, he gained his old strength back, and Foley was amazed at how well the wounds healed. He had never seen anything like it in all of his hospital work. He considered O'Brien's recovery a small miracle.

Spaulding was a one-street town, and in the next week O'Brien began walking the length of that one street, getting his legs under him. He finally stopped hurting so much inside, and his healed lung was back to pretty much full capacity. Foley had removed some chipped-off bone from the ribs, and that was all healing well, too.

In less than sixty days, O'Brien was well. He was doing strength exercises out behind the cabin, getting muscle back. He went to a small store in

Spaulding and outfitted himself again with boots and clean rawhides. Foley cut some of his long hair off and O'Brien trimmed the handlebar mustache. He looked almost like he had on that fateful day of the ambush now, except he had lost some tan from his square face. He found that the gear and belongings on the Appaloosa's irons had been undisturbed, so he still had two rifles, one of them the buffalo gun. He purchased another big hunting knife and fitted it to his right boot in a sheath inside the boot, as he had done before, and he figured he was ready to take up the hunt for Luther Gabriel again. He still had some gold pieces that had been secreted on his mount's irons, and one day he dropped several of them into Foley's hand.

"This is for everything you done for me," he said to Foley at the cabin door. O'Brien had just come in from saddling the Appaloosa, and it stood patiently out in the sun, waiting for him. "I know it ain't enough, but I'm a man of limited means."

"You didn't have to pay me nothing, O'Brien," Foley told him.

O'Brien smiled and placed a big hand on Foley's shoulder. "I won't never forget you, old man."

"I guess you'll be looking for them what bushwhacked you," Foley said.

O'Brien nodded. "That's been on my mind some."

"Well, I hope your luck holds up through it, hunter," Foley offered.

O'Brien nodded. A few minutes later, he was

boarding the mottled gray horse, bidding Foley farewell. He reckoned he would never see him again.

O'Brien figured on riding into Douglas to do some asking about Gabriel. But first he had a visit to make. He rode out to the ambush site at the rock outcroppings, and he found Sumner's shallow grave out there.

O'Brien was not a sentimental man, but it choked him up some to look down on that final resting place of Wesley Sumner. O'Brien had felt as close to that gunfighter as he had to anyone in recent years, including Aaron Seger.

O'Brien took his new hat off, a dark brown, wide-brimmed Stetson, and his shaggy hair moved in a warm breeze. He regarded the mound of dirt grimly.

"It ain't over, bounty hunter," he said in a quiet voice. "I promise you that. That bastard's name was Mudd from that hellish day he done this to us.

"I swear it on your grave."

Chapter Twelve

Luther Gabriel, meanwhile, had moved on into New Mexico.

Gabriel intended to make himself a temporary headquarters at Socorro, partway between Albuquerque and Las Cruces. There was a small farm for sale south of Socorro, and it had a house on it that would fill his need. He would operate out of that, getting rid of all law south and west of there, then installing his people as the only authority. Old Man Clanton had shown him how in Arizona. Clanton had killed off and bought off all the law in those parts except for the newly arrived Earps, and even they had not curtailed Clanton's power in that area. Gabriel could do the same thing in New Mexico.

He had some money in an Albuquerque bank but not enough to do things the way he wanted to. He wanted to purchase the small farm outright, and that was going to take some cash. So Gabriel's next step was to plan a bank robbery in Silver City on his way back to Socorro.

Gabriel had also done some further recruiting on the way, and now had three more men with him, tough drifters who were interested only in immediate gain but who made Gabriel believe they were as power hungry as he.

Gabriel had found another temporary head-quarters outside Silver City to house his growing troops while he tried to make their capital grow. A ranch house outside of town a few miles had been torn down when the property was sold, and a hunter had purchased the bunkhouse for a hunting lodge. But then he had fallen ill, and the bunkhouse had fallen into disuse. Gabriel found out about it and paid a month's rent to house his men there until he was ready to move on.

The bunkhouse was a long one-room affair with a dozen bunks along two walls and a stove, table, and chairs that had been put there by the hunter. It was a perfect setup for Gabriel's temporary stay while he plotted against the town's bank. It even had a thrown-together outhouse at the rear and a hitching rail at the front entrance. It was small for ten men, but Gabriel did not figure on being there long.

It was on a dry, dusty August day that Gabriel took all nine of his underlings into Silver City to rob its only bank. When the gang rode together now, they were formidable. No sheriff or marshal could stand against them alone or with a deputy or two. They were too powerful a force, just as the James gang had been for so many years, until Jesse rode into Northfield, Minnesota. Gabriel assured himself, though, that there was no Northfield massacre in his future. Jesse had let his guard down and had paid the price. Anyway, Gabriel's future did not depend on robbing banks. With a little luck, he would become a legitimate force in New Mexico in time. Then he would bleed its citizens dry.

The locals of Silver City looked up in wariness when all ten of the Gabriel gang rode in that morning, their mounts' hooves making a slight rumbling sound like distant thunder. The only law in Silver City was a middle-aged sheriff who kept an office down the dirt street a block from the bank, and he was a marked man that hot morning.

The riders stopped before the bank, and Gabriel regarded the building sternly. Beside him was Cuesta, and Purcell sat his mount right behind those two. The bank was a stucco affair with a high false front and bars on its windows. A clerk inside had just raised shades in those windows and unlocked the big front door. The bank was ready for business.

"Cuesta, go find the sheriff," Gabriel said quietly. "Take Skinner with you."

They were all dismounting now, except for Cuesta and the barrel-chested fellow called Skinner, the gunman who thought he had killed O'Brien. They rode down the street and dismounted before the sheriff's office, which was also the jail. Cuesta nodded to Skinner, and they went on inside.

The sheriff was nailing a wanted dodger to the far wall when they walked in. Both of them drew their guns before he turned, and when he saw them, his eyes widened.

"What's going on, boys?"

There was a strong odor of coffee brewing, coming from a back room, and somebody had placed a glass of fall flowers on the sheriff's scarred, weatherbeaten desk to their right. It was a rather pleasant, homey scene.

"You the sheriff hereabouts?" Cuesta asked in his accent.

"Why, yes," the sheriff replied, eyeing the guns. "Can I help you boys with something?"

"Just by getting out of our way, old man," Skinner grated out.

Then both of them fired several shots into the man wearing the badge. Their guns banged loudly in the small whitewashed room, making explosion after explosion, and the sheriff's body jerked and jumped about on the far wall, and finally slid to the floor, leaving crimson stains as he went. He had been dead before he fell.

Cuesta glanced at Skinner. "Come on, let's go join the fiesta, my friend."

At the bank, several men stayed outside while Gabriel, Purcell, and two Clanton men went inside. They did not try to hide their faces in any way. They just bulled their way in with guns drawn, and Gabriel pushed his Schofield .45 up into the face of the nearest teller. "We want everything in the safe," he said simply. "Your sheriff is dead, and you can't count on any miracles. I suggest you do what you have to to get us what we want."

There were only two customers present, an old man and a stout woman. They both stepped aside and hoped for the best. In the meantime, the young male teller was not understanding the importance of what he had just been told.

"The vault hasn't been opened yet, sir," he said to Gabriel. "I don't know the combination, and the only officer here is out back in the—"

Gabriel's Schofield went off in the middle of that sentence, making everybody's ears ring and blowing a hole in the teller's shirt front. The young man went tripping backwards, arms flying, and struck a desk of a young woman behind him. His form slid across the desk, taking papers with it, and fell to the floor on the far side, almost knocking the woman clerk down. She saw the blood on the desk and screamed. Purcell went through a gate and stuck a gun up onto her right breast.

"Shut up, lady!"

The officer the first teller had been referring to had now emerged from a rear door, white-faced. Gabriel went over to him. "This ain't no game we're playing here, mister. Open that safe up. Now."

It required only a few minutes to follow Gabriel's orders, then Gabriel and Purcell were in the big safe. There were bags of silver, some gold, and a lot of paper money and bonds. It was more than Gabriel thought, and he was very pleased.

"Okay, boys. We got what we come for. Let's ride."

On their way past the stout female customer,

though, she came and stood brazenly before Gabriel. He held his revolver in his right hand and two bags of coins in the other.

"You shot that boy down in cold blood! Do you think there is no justice in God's creation? Do you really think you can just ride out of here and never answer for so foul a deed, you filthy scum?"

Gabriel was going to just brush on past her until she called him the name. He raised the muzzle of the Schofield and squeezed the trigger again. The woman was picked up and dropped like a bag of grain, shot through the heart. The two Clanton cowpokes eyed each other darkly, and Purcell just stared down at her for a long moment. Gabriel did not notice.

"Let's clear this place!" he growled.

O'Brien had found out almost immediately that Gabriel had headed back east into New Mexico from Douglas. He also learned that Gabriel had hired himself a gang again and that he had bullied the local sheriff. O'Brien bought some supplies in Douglas and drank some rye whiskey, then rode on out the way he had come in, through the pass where he and Sumner had been ambushed, past Sumner's grave site, and on east.

On the first couple of nights on the trail, O'Brien cleaned the two rifles on his mount's irons and got the Remington sawed-off shotgun out of his bedroll behind his saddle. That had been spared as well as the rifles, and he had purchased more ammunition for it and them in Douglas.

O'Brien had no plan about how he should go after Gabriel once he caught up with him. He would play it along as the cards were dealt to him, the way he always had hunted buffalo. If you made definite plans based on one set of circumstances, you might not be pliable if the circumstances were not as expected. So you assessed reality first, then acted.

It was on the day after Gabriel had robbed the bank in Silver City that O'Brien heard about him again. O'Brien had ridden into a tiny town called White Signal, just west of Silver City, and was having supper in a saloon-café, when he spotted the fellow at the next table reading a newspaper. O'Brien saw big headlines that he found he could read:

"GANG ROBS SILVER CITY BANK."

He rose and went over to the other table. "Say, mister. Ain't that telling about a bank robbery east of here?"

The fellow was a store clerk who did not like the looks of O'Brien. He looked O'Brien over arrogantly. "Yes, it is."

"Would you read some of that article to me?" O'Brien said. He hated to admit he could not read well.

The fellow laughed in his throat. "I'm eating at the moment, sir. If you'll be patient, I'll allow you to look at the paper when I've finished."

O'Brien's patience did not go far these days. He reached down and picked the thin fellow up by the shirt front and lifted him clear off the floor, knocking his chair over. "Do you hear right?" he growled.

The clerk was terrified. "I'll . . . read it! Just put . . . me down!"

O'Brien set him back on the chair, and the clerk got a better hold on the newspaper and himself. He looked warily from O'Brien to the paper. "It says the Silver City Bank was robbed by a gang of close to a dozen men. They killed two people at the bank, and they also killed the sheriff. Some fellow in a black beard seemed to be the leader."

"Luther Gabriel," O'Brien muttered darkly.

"That's about all, except that the gang is still in the area. There's no law to do anything about it, though."

O'Brien nodded. "How far is Silver City from here?"

"Why, it's just a day's ride," the clerk said. He looked up at O'Brien's square, rugged face. "Are you a lawman, stranger?"

O'Brien glanced down at him for a moment. "Much obliged for your help," he said acidly. Then he turned and left the place. He would ride out for Silver City before tomorrow's sun was up.

O'Brien did not sleep well that night. He had the white buffalo dream again, and now Gabriel was riding its shaggy back, as it ran roughshod over little Annie Seger, Aaron, then Certainty Sumner. And O'Brien was firing the big Sharps like a Gatling gun, and the bullets were going right through the animal and through Gabriel.

O'Brien did not seem to feel the loss of rest, though. Something inside him was wired tight now. He was up in the dark, saddling the Appaloosa, and was off for Silver City in morning blackness. He arrived there in early afternoon.

The place was like a morgue. Up at the local boot hill they were burying the sheriff when O'Brien arrived, and he rode on up there and stood through the brief ceremony. A black-frocked minister was saying some words over the open grave.

"The first man is out of the Earth and is made of dust. The second man is out of Heaven and is spiritual. And just as we have borne the image of the one made of dust, so shall we bear also the image of the heavenly one."

It was a grim ceremony, one that O'Brien knew had been preceded by many others where Gabriel had roamed. Sheriffs and marshals were a dying breed in Gabriel territory. O'Brien watched while the casket was lowered into the grave, and then it was over. He walked over to the minister.

"The paper said that the men who did this are still hereabouts," O'Brien said. "Where are they?"

The pale-faced man looked suddenly very afraid. "None of that is any of my business, mister. Now, please excuse me."

The man walked off, dispersing with the rest of the small gathering. O'Brien shook his head. If Gabriel ever got really established somewhere, fear would protect him as much as his guns.

He led the Appaloosa back down the hill and into town, and saw all the crepe hanging about. A bulletin board announced the funerals of the bank teller and the woman customer for the following day. It was all very somber.

O'Brien went into the saloon across the street from the Silver City Bank and ordered a whiskey at the bar there. He swigged it down in one gulp while the bartender busied himself at the shelves behind the counter. Finally, O'Brien spoke to him.

"That's a bad thing that happened here," he said.

The bartender turned to him. He was almost as big as O'Brien, but most of his weight was fat. He was a robust, red-faced fellow who looked like a butcher.

"Yeah. Too bad." He had sold the gang a lot of liquor, had liked their business, and was privately glad they had not left yet for farther east.

"I hear the people that did the killing are still in the area," O'Brien said, watching the other man's beefy face.

The bartender glanced at him. "Oh, yeah?"

O'Brien knew in that instant that the bartender knew their whereabouts. He placed a seated Liberty quarter on the bar for the drink and looked up at the other man.

"Where are they holed up?" O'Brien said.

The barkeep shook his head. "You don't ask questions like that, stranger. If I knew, I couldn't tell you."

O'Brien shook his shaggy head under the Stetson. He got up off his stool, came around the bar at its far end, and walked down to the bartender.

"Hey. You ain't allowed back here," the other fellow said quickly. He grabbed a short wooden club and wielded it against O'Brien's purposeful approach. "You get to hell out, or you bought yourself a cracked skull."

In the last few feet, he did finally swing the club. O'Brien caught it easily in his left hand, then twisted it forcibly from the bartender's grasp. O'Brien then swung it backhanded at the other man, and it caught him across the side of the head. The beefy man went crashing against the shelves, breaking glass there, then fell, grunting to the floor. O'Brien kicked him in the side and then in the back. The other man yelled, and then there was only groaning. O'Brien threw the club to the floor.

"Now, I'll try again. Where are they?"

The other man rolled onto his back, barely conscious. "You're a goddam wild . . . animal."

"Where are they?" O'Brien said ominously.

The bartender wiped at blood running down the side of his head. He could hardly see. "There's an old bunkhouse south of town a few miles. On the old Spencer place. I hear they're holed up out there. But I can't vouch for it."

All the dislike of townspeople boiled up in O'Brien in that moment, and he hated their weakness, selfishness, and dishonor. He hauled off and savagely kicked the bartender once more in the side, and a rib audibly cracked under the blow. The bartender yelled out a new, terrified cry.

"Now, wasn't that easy?" O'Brien said in a deep growl.

He stormed out of the place then, busting one of the swinging doors off its hinges as he left.

That afternoon, before it got dark, O'Brien went to the local store and bought up a small load of dynamite and fuses. He had heard from a person on the street that the bold gang had already come into town to drink since the shootings and robbery, and that they were expected back that evening. That was another reason why the town looked so dead: everybody was afraid to be caught out on the street when the killers returned.

O'Brien slowly formulated his plan. He knew that he could not just go after Gabriel now but had to take the whole gang down. These men could make Quantrill's Raiders seem like church parsons. O'Brien would get them all. Or go down trying.

So he waited.

The sun set slowly. The heat of the midday dispersed, and he waited some more.

Finally, it was dark.

An hour after dark, they came.

It was Gabriel himself whom O'Brien recognized from posters. All the other men were there, too, except for barrel-chested Skinner and Purcell. O'Brien stood in a doorway and watched them ride past, taking no action against them. They all dismounted boldly and noisily, entering the saloon where O'Brien had beaten information from the barkeep earlier. The beefy man had been replaced by a subordinate, and O'Brien had warned both of them that they should not mention him to the gang.

When they were all inside, O'Brien mounted the Appaloosa and rode out to the bunkhouse.

It was only a short ride out there. You could see the place at a distance, because it was all lighted up. O'Brien approached slowly, watching for trouble. There were two mounts hitched to the rail out front, because Skinner and Purcell had been left there to act as guards.

O'Brien dismounted from the Appaloosa a hundred yards from the building in a small stand of cottonwoods. It was a clear, hot night, and his figure cast a shadow on the hard ground. A small groan issued from his throat as he reached for the double-barreled Remington, because the chest wound still gave him pain inside him, and his face felt hot because he still had periodic fevers from that same healing wound. He knew he was not the man he had been before the ambush, and he was not sure he ever would be, but there was no delaying what he had to do or try to do. He could not live with himself if he turned his back on Luther Gabriel after what he had done to the people that mattered to O'Brien.

He retrieved the dynamite sticks and fuses from the saddlery, too, and then he walked the hundred yards to the building. He put the dynamite down near the entrance to the place and looked inside. Purcell was seated at the table in the center of the long room, reading a dime novel. A bottle of whiskey stood near him on the table. O'Brien did not recognize Purcell as one of the ambush party, because he had never gotten a look at him on that hot, deadly day. O'Brien peered around the rest of the room and did not see another man. He moved from the window and around to the side of the building, saw the outhouse back there and heard a low cough come from it. He returned to the front door.

It was all over for Purcell and Skinner in the next sixty seconds. O'Brien kicked savagely at the front door, and the entire wood-plank fixture went crashing inward, banging on the floor inside the room. Then O'Brien was standing on it, the shotgun out in front of him, a low growl issuing from his throat, like a grizzly about to attack.

Purcell jumped visibly at the crash, then turned and stared hard at O'Brien, recognizing him immediately. The look on his narrow, bony face turned from surprise to deep shock.

"Holy Mother of God! You're . . . dead!"

O'Brien made no reply. In the next moment, which seemed like an eternity to Purcell, he rose awkwardly from the straight chair and went for his gun. While his hand was still at the holster, though, the thick shotgun blasted out in the confines of the room, shaking its timbers. Purcell was hit in mid-chest, and his heart was exploded like a desert melon. He was thrown to the floor hard and was still twitching and jumping there as O'Brien strode over to him and to the back door, kicking it wide open and busting one of its plank boards.

Skinner, the barrel-chested gunman who had fired off a round into O'Brien's chest with O'Brien down and almost gone on that ambush day, was just emerging from the outhouse wide-eyed, pulling up on his trousers, which were around his hips. He stopped in mid-stride as O'Brien stepped down from the doorway and aimed the shotgun in his direction. In that timeless moment, Skinner recognized the buffalo hunter.

"Maybe I come at a bad time," O'Brien growled.

"It can't be!" Skinner whispered.

The shotgun answered him. He was hit in the

low chest and blown back into the open doorway of the outhouse behind him, hitting the door frame with both arms and fracturing them as he went.

When O'Brien went and looked into the small building, he saw Skinner slouched there on a toilet seat, his face all twisted up and working, as if he were in the middle of a particularly difficult bowel movement. There was blood and ripped flesh everywhere.

O'Brien raised a hinged part of the seat beside Skinner and leaned it against the back wall of the place. Then he tipped Skinner over, while Skinner's jaw was still working, and dumped him unceremoniously into the excrement pit below, head first. There was some gurgling down there for a moment, and then it was quiet.

Now O'Brien had some work cut out for himself. He went inside and hauled out the corpse of Purcell, dragged it into the outhouse, and dumped it into the pit on top of Skinner. Then he closed the lid down.

"Thought you boys might enjoy resting in your natural element," he growled under his breath.

His next job was a more lengthy one. He noted that the bunkhouse, like so many structures of the south country, was set up off the ground on concrete pilings. Now, at intervals, he placed eight dynamite charges underneath the perimeter of the building and began affixing fuses to the bundles. That took most of an hour, and he kept watching for the return of the men from town, but they did not come. Lastly, he ran all the shorter fuses into a juncture about ten yards from the building, then kicked some dirt up onto the exposed fuses. He stuck an unused dynamite stick into his belt, at his waist, in case he needed it later.

The two horses picketed to the hitching rail were acting very skittery and jumpy, so he had a decision to make. Whether to have the men see no horses when they came or two very nervous ones. O'Brien chose the former. He untethered the two mounts, slapped them on their rumps, and drove them off. They galloped away into the night.

He returned to the Appaloosa, which was well hidden in the trees, got the Winchester rifle off its irons, and reloaded the Remington shotgun. He was ready. He returned to a position about twenty-five yards from the building, behind some low rocks, and hid himself there. He would wait again now, as he had done so often. Hiding from a herd. Blending into the background.

The night passed slowly, and a full moon climbed higher in the black sky. Soon it would be the hunter's moon, and O'Brien had to wonder if he would really be out there again, tracking shaggies. He stared at the empty building where oil lamps burned brightly for no one. The moon climbed higher. A horned owl hooted forlornly from a nearby cottonwood. A lone coyote wailed out a lonesome call into the blackness.

Then came the distant tremble of hoofbeats.

They would have been inaudible to most ears, but O'Brien had learned to hear things that other men could not. The riders were about a mile off.

A few minutes later they came into sight, black silhouettes under the moon. They were laughing and talking and having a good time. With no law in the area now, they had no fear. Earlier in the evening, the Clanton man with the transparent eyebrows and baby face had raped a woman in her home. Another, one of the more recent recruits, had beaten an older man so badly outside the saloon that he was still unconscious.

They were having a great time.

They straggled in by ones and twos, some of them tipping flasks to their mouths. Gabriel and Cuesta came in almost side by side. O'Brien could have killed Gabriel as Gabriel passed within fifteen yards of him, but he chose not to. He wanted them all.

Now the front runners had stopped at the hitching rail, and Gabriel had already noticed that the two mounts of Purcell and Skinner were gone.

"What the hell!" O'Brien heard Gabriel say in his raspy voice. "Where are their horses? Are they in there?"

"I can't tell, Luther," Cuesta's voice came. "I'll check it out."

Cuesta was dismounting ahead of Gabriel, and Gabriel was now eyeing the surrounding area warily. Most of the others had arrived and were dismounting, too, picketing their mounts. Cuesta drew his sidearm and went up to the front entrance. Sumner had described Cuesta to O'Brien, and O'Brien now recognized him, too. O'Brien had reaffixed the front door to its hinges and just stood it up wide open, and Cuesta noticed no damage when he entered the place.

He came back out in a moment, and now a couple of others had drawn guns. "They are not there, *compadre*," he reported to Gabriel. "But everything looks okay."

"I heard Skinner mention some farm near here," O'Brien could hear Gabriel saying. "I'll bet them two went to hooraw some locals. Sonofabitch." He dismounted, too, and picketed his mount. Cuesta and the others reholstered their guns, and O'Brien, from behind the boulders, let out a long breath.

One by one they filed into the building, including Gabriel. The night was still hot, and they left the door open, still not noticing the damage. O'Brien's luck was holding.

In just moments, they were all inside. Two of them went out to the outhouse, and O'Brien waited again. But then the two straggled back without having discovered the bodies out there. The ex-sergeant from the Clanton bunch came out and untethered the eight mounts and led them to a small fenced area behind the outhouse and corraled them there, unsaddling them. By now several of the gang had hit their bunks, but O'Brien could see a lot of movement inside and could hear Gabriel's voice. Finally the ex-sergeant returned to the house through the rear door.

O'Brien made his move.

As he had done so many times on the hunt, he came on his belly, the Winchester in one hand and the Remington in the other. Halfway there, the dumpy, red-faced Clanton man came to the front entrance and spat onto the ground, then stood and looked around for a moment. He was wearing no shirt. O'Brien was right out in the open and only yards away. He flattened himself to the ground, motionless, and did not breathe. The fellow finally turned and went back inside.

O'Brien crawled the rest of the way to the fuse junction and got a match out of his rawhides. He was about a dozen yards from the front of the building and off to one side. He could hear some talking from inside the place.

"You ought to heard her yell when I begun tearing them pretty clothes off her." Some laughter.

"Maybe I'll have to try me that tomorrow night."

"We won't be here tomorrow night." Gabriel's voice. "We're heading east tomorrow. We're attracting too much attention hereabouts. I'll double our strength by the time we reach Socorro."

O'Brien suddenly realized, lying out there on his belly, that he could not let this opportunity pass. He had to succeed tonight—or maybe never.

He rose onto one knee and struck the match, lighting the fuses.

They all began fizzing and traveling toward the building at about the same rate of speed. One fizzled, then started up again. All eight were burning.

O'Brien regained his feet and was starting to return to cover when another gunman showed up at the front doorway. He looked right at O'Brien, and his face changed.

"Hey! Who the hell are you?" He was a rather muscular-looking fellow, one of the last recruited. He immediately went for a gun on his hip, and O'Brien saw the movement.

O'Brien reluctantly raised the muzzle of the Winchester and fired. The rifle barked out clearly in the warm night and punched the gunman back against the doorjamb. The slug had hit him dead center, and as he slid to the threshold, his eyes were already wide and unseeing.

There was some yelling from inside, and O'Brien was swearing under his breath. He abandoned his idea of going for cover and circled around to face the front door. Two men appeared there, one in front of the other. The first one aimed a gun at O'Brien and fired. It was Baby Face, the rapist.

O'Brien felt the tug of the hot lead at his left arm, but the bullet had just grazed his flesh. He still held both guns, so was firing the rifle one-handed. It banged out again, and the Clanton man yelled and fell against the man behind him.

Then the whole world seemed to erupt in a violent series of thunderous explosions. Yellow flashes brightened the blackness of the night as the bunkhouse appeared to disintegrate into a sudden Hades. Wood boards and timbers sailed through the air, and one came at O'Brien like a lance and missed his head by the width of a .44 slug. O'Brien was thrown wildly off his feet and lost the rifle but held onto the shotgun.

As he lay on his back in the dirt, hat gone, ears ringing, he watched the bunkhouse catch fire and begin blazing in the dark, what was left of it. Cuesta came stumbling out the front of the place, his left leg ablaze, his left arm blown away. He spotted O'Brien and squinted down on him. *"The hunter!"* he croaked out. *"The goddam . . . hunter!"*

He aimed his Mauser at O'Brien, and O'Brien rolled over once to his right, and the shot dug up sand beside him. He came up on his back firing, the shotgun blasting out its own booming message, and Cuesta was hit in the crotch. He was yelling even before he hit the ground, but it did not last long. He died in moments.

O'Brien regained his feet. The building was flaming terribly, and black smoke now curled into the inkiness of the sky. Inside the bunkhouse, there was some screaming as the two new recruits and the remaining others caught fire, a couple of them already half-dead from the explosions, limbs torn and flesh mauled. The dumpy, red-faced Clanton gunman came running awkwardly out of the place afire, a living torch. There was a hole in his right side from the explosion. He ran right at O'Brien and fell to the ground almost at O'Brien's feet. Flames still burned him. He looked up at O'Brien through a charred face. "Help . . . me!"

O'Brien just stared hard at him. The fellow collapsed onto his face and was dead.

O'Brien wanted to make sure of Gabriel. He made a wide circuit around the flaming hulk of the building and could see some dark figures in there on the floor, burning. He shaded his eyes, staring in there. Then he heard the gravelly voice behind him.

"I don't believe it."

O'Brien turned quickly and saw the Schofield aimed at his heart. Standing behind the wicked-looking revolver was Luther Gabriel. His right leg below the knee was bloody, and the side of his bearded face was burned. But he had been thrown clear of the fire, and O'Brien had not seen him back near the outhouse. O'Brien felt the shotgun in his right hand but remembered now that he had pulled off both rounds at Cuesta and the gun was empty.

He had made a second mistake against Gabriel, and now it looked like it was Gabriel's card game. O'Brien felt a hollowness rise into his gut.

"They said they'd killed you," Gabriel grated out. His voice sounded as if it had been dredged up from a sewer.

"They was wrong," O'Brien said heavily. There was absolutely no way out of this. Gabriel was an excellent shot; the slightest movement from O'Brien would send a hot slug into his chest. He was finished. Gabriel had won.

"You scalped my goddam brother," Gabriel was saying in that hard voice. "And now you ruined what I had going here. A bullet's too good for you, you bastard."

O'Brien grunted. "Just get it done, Gabriel."

Gabriel looked at O'Brien's belt at his waist and saw the stick of dynamite there that O'Brien had not used when setting the explosives around the building. It was stuck vertically into O'Brien's thick belt, the fuse pointing up.

Gabriel's hard eyes narrowed down. "Drop the shotgun," he said breathlessly.

O'Brien frowned slightly. "Why should I?"

"Drop the goddam shotgun!" Gabriel screamed at him crazily.

O'Brien remembered something Sumner had said once, about how delay could change the odds when they were against you. He hesitated and dropped the gun to the ground. Its only use was as a club, anyway.

"Now light that fuse," Gabriel gritted out, grimacing and taking the weight off his bloody leg.

"Huh?" O'Brien said.

"You heard me. You got matches left. Light the fuse on that powder stick but leave it in your belt."

O'Brien started some game playing. "Go to hell," he said.

"If you don't, buffalo man, I'll start on your kneecaps, your groin, and your elbows. I'll shoot you into little pieces. Slow like." Gabriel would have, too, but he was too scared of O'Brien to try. He had heard the stories about him.

O'Brien sighed and got a match out of a rawhide pocket.

"That's right. Now light the fuse," Gabriel said.

O'Brien struck the match on his belt, hesitated, and then touched it to the end of the six-inch fuse. It began fizzing and burning.

"Now let's see how many parts of you will be left when that fuse burns down," Gabriel grinned feverishly.

O'Brien returned the grin and began walking toward Gabriel. It was a slow-burning fuse, and he had about two minutes. Gabriel's eyes widened slightly. "Hold it!" he yelled.

O'Brien took another step forward. "Maybe there will be more parts flying around than you thought, Gabriel. You sure you ain't too close?" He gambled and took another step toward Gabriel. He was suddenly ten feet away. He closed it to eight.

Gabriel's face changed. He glanced at the fuse, and it was almost halfway down. "Stay back, damn you!"

"What for?" O'Brien grinned. "You going to shoot me, Gabriel?" He took another step closer.

Gabriel panicked, took a quick step backwards on uneven ground, and the bad leg gave way on him. In the next instant, he was falling to the ground.

O'Brien dived at him then, and the Schofield went off as Gabriel pulled the trigger in desperation. The bullet tore up rawhide under O'Brien's arm, and then he was grabbing at Gabriel and the gun. There was a lot of grunting and straining there for a moment, and the gun went flying, and then O'Brien's big fist thudded against Gabriel's jaw, stunning him.

O'Brien yanked the dynamite stick from his belt. The fuse was burnt almost to the top of the stick. O'Brien jammed the thing into Gabriel's shirt, broke loose from Gabriel, and rolled away.

When Gabriel realized what had happened and heard the fizzing of the dynamite inside his shirt, he began tearing at the cloth to get at it as O'Brien rolled farther from blast center. *"No!"* Gabriel was yelling. *"God, no!"*

But God did not intervene. The explosion came an instant later when O'Brien had put twenty feet between them, crawling the last couple of yards. His ears were punched hard by the blast, and the night flashed yellow for a moment, and when O'Brien looked, there were pieces of Gabriel raining down all over the compound. An arm banged up against the outhouse, the lower torso and a leg sailed into the guttering ruins of the bunkhouse, and a bloody head and chest hit the dirt beyond O'Brien.

There was almost nothing left of Gabriel. O'Brien struggled unsteadily to his feet, his ears still ringing like clamorous church bells. He staggered foward, then stood above the head of Luther Gabriel, and Gabriel's eyes were wide open, bulging from their sockets. It was all very messy. And satisfying.

"I should of told you, trail dung," O'Brien said quietly to the lifeless head at his feet. "A bear ain't dead till you got him skinned."

He went and laboriously retrieved the Remington nearby, took one last look at Gabriel, and headed back around the low-burning bunkhouse.

Now Aaron Seger could rest in peace.

And all the others that Gabriel had mauled, molested, and murdered.

As for Certainty Sumner, O'Brien hoped there was just some small corner of the Good Place for men who hunted other men for bounties on their heads.

That didn't seem like much to ask.

Epilogue

O'Brien's new wounds from the Silver City shootout healed rather quickly. The deep one, though, in his chest from the Douglas ambush continued to bother him quite a bit, especially whenever a blue norther would spring up on the horizon.

Certainty Sumner had had no relatives that O'Brien knew of, but the bounty hunter had confided to O'Brien one dark night in hardship camp that he had always hoped to be buried in some civilized place like Kansas City. So O'Brien exhumed his friend's body, put it in a wooden casket, and hauled it to Albuquerque in a hide wagon. There he paid to give Sumner a real burial in a pleasant-looking place. He knew Sumner had had some good drinking bouts in Albuquerque and hoped he would have found the site appropriate.

While O'Brien was in Albuquerque, and before he got back to any real hunting, he visited Annie again at the private hospital for which he and

Sumner had paid earlier.

He had a pleasant surprise.

Annie had responded to treatment in the new, better facility and was anticipating his visit with real happiness. O'Brien had cleaned himself up and even ran a comb through his long, shaggy hair, but hospital staff regarded him darkly in the corridors and avoided close contact with him. The doctor in charge was more personable, however, than the one at the state facility and was pleased that O'Brien had come to see Annie.

She was standing in a whitewashed, sunny room with flowers in a vase on an oak table when O'Brien found her. She looked thinner, but a little taller, and even though there was a paleness to her complexion, she looked healthy.

"O'Brien!" she said warmly when he came in.

An attendant left them alone. Annie came and shook O'Brien's hand, and he missed the kiss on the cheek she used to give him. But that would come, in time.

"It pleases me to see you so well, Annie," he told her.

"I wondered if you'd come back. They say I can leave here one of these days soon."

"Well, there's no hurry about it. I gave the doctor some more money, so you're here as long as you have to be."

They spoke awkwardly at first, and most of it was about the past and Aaron. She never mentioned the rape.

"I don't know where I'll go from here," she said nonchalantly.

O'Brien nodded. "I know that's been on your

mind. The doctor just got a letter back from your aunt back in Memphis, Annie. She wants you back there with her."

Annie was surprised. "I don't really know her."

"Her and your mother was real close," O'Brien said. "You'll like it back there, Annie. It's better for a young lady."

She paused. She had hoped O'Brien would take her. It sounded wonderful to her to go out on the trail hunting. But she realized it was a childish hope: "I reckon so," she said.

"I already paid the doctor your fare back there," O'Brien went on. "You'll be leaving here within sixty days. I'm real proud of you, Annie. And I know Aaron would be."

"You'll always be my best friend, O'Brien," she said.

O'Brien nodded, smiling behind the long mustache.

"I wanted you to thank that other fellow, too, that come with you at the other place."

O'Brien knew she meant Sumner. He nodded. "I'll tell him," he said.

O'Brien felt good after that visit. Things had worked out fairly well at the end. It was Luther Gabriel that was pushing up daisies at Silver City and not him. O'Brien figured the myth about Gabriel and the white buffalo was just that—a bunch of nonsense.

Then he walked into the lobby of the Bank of New Mexico to withdraw some funds he had stashed there.

It caught his eye the moment he walked in the door. The enormous, white buffalo robe. Hanging on a high wall where the world could see it.

He walked over to it and just stared. The robe had been fluffed and currycombed and prettied up until it dazzled the eye. But it was off the devil beast: O'Brien would have recognized it among a thousand.

"I'll be a sonofabitch," he muttered.

A bank guard came up beside him. "What do you think, mister? It's a real beauty, isn't it?"

O'Brien did not look at him. He was remembering that hot day when the animal had almost killed him, and Certainty Sumner had saved his skin.

"Yeah," he said. "Nice."

"A hunter named Wiley took a whole gang with him up into the mountains, and they finally killed it. It was a killer, you know. Seven men it done away with, all hunters. It took five of them to bring it down. The governor called it a miracle."

O'Brien nodded absently.

"They say that Wiley is the best there is. Say, maybe you'd know, you look like a hunter yourself."

"Wiley's a goddam spring-trap, crazy greenhorn that fired on a herd once with a Gatling," O'Brien said more to himself than the guard. "Even McGraw was better than Wiley."

The guard's face had gone sober. "I see."

O'Brien turned to him, not knowing if he wanted to hear the reply to the question he was about to ask. "Can you tell me when this animal was killed?" he said.

The guard nodded. "Sure. They say Wiley brought it down on September 3."

O'Brien did a quick calculation, then began shaking his shaggy head slowly. "I'll be damned," he said to himself.

"Huh?" the guard said.

O'Brien turned to him. "That night outside Silver City. That all happened in the early morning of the 4th, just after midnight of the 3rd."

The guard scratched his chin. "I don't mean to throw mud on no one, mister, but you aren't making much sense."

Now O'Brien would never know for sure. Whether the Indian's charm on Gabriel was real, whether Gabriel would have allowed O'Brien that last-minute slack at the burning building on that flaming night, whether Gabriel would be alive now and rebuilding to take over this territory, and O'Brien would be a charred corpse there at Silver City if it had all happened on September 2. It was all a little unnerving. In O'Brien's business, a man liked to rely on his own skills and survival instinct, and not have to worry that some goddam Blackfoot could influence the outcome of events by chanting words and shaking bones in a bag.

"Uh, forget it," O'Brien said.

"Maybe you'd like to open an account," the guard was saying. "Or make a withdrawal?"

But O'Brien was already on his way out of the place. He could take the money out later. Right now, he needed a drink. Off by himself.

Where he could drive the white buffalo out of his head and remember those good nights on the trail with Certainty Sumner reading to him from the newspaper.

Where he could remember. And forget.